A Pie For A Pie

Copyright © 2024 by London Lovett

All rights reserved.

No part of this book may be reproduced in any form or by any electronic or mechanical means, including information storage and retrieval systems, without written permission from the author, except for the use of brief quotations in a book review.

ISBN: 9798340480408

Imprint: Independently published

A Scottie Ramone Cozy Mystery

A Pie for a Pie

LONDON LOVETT

one
. . .

"I'VE ALWAYS BEEN a big fan of pumpkin pie, but after baking sixteen of them in a single morning, I think I'll bake a cherry pie for Thanksgiving." Jack wiped his thick hands off with the towel hanging from his apron. "I'm going to smell like cinnamon and cloves for the rest of the weekend." He shrugged. "I suppose I could smell worse."

I laughed as I set the mixing bowls in the sink. "Being the only bakery in town, I suppose I should have anticipated the pie order for the annual pie eating contest. Thanks for finishing those." My gaze swept across the line of perfectly baked pies. Jack could roll and shape pie crust with the precision of a machine. He'd spent some of his baking years in an industrial setting, which gave him the skills to bake uniform products at a high volume, but he was also an artist, who, given time and ingredients, created beautiful pastries and cakes that could compete with master pastry chefs. I'd been one of those highly-sought-after pastry chefs at one time, but I'd found my true happiness back in my quaint hometown of Ripple Creek. Now I baked for pleasure and not under the watchful, critical eye of restaurant owners and food critics.

Jack had gone through some rough times and ended up in jail for a short stint. He'd asked me to give him a chance, and giving him that chance turned out to be the best decision in my baking career. We were a perfect team.

I filled the sink with warm, soapy water and glanced out to the front of the shop. It was empty. The locals and regular customers had already swept through for their morning treats and bread loaves. The summer crowds were long gone, and once the chill of fall had taken hold, even the late summer/early fall vacationers had left. The landscape no longer held the bright, glorious splashes of yellows and gold that exploded in the colorful peak of autumn. The aspens had begun to shed their coin-shaped leaves, and the nip in the air whispered warnings of the coming winter.

I personally loved this time of year, when hot soup and warm knit scarves were essential, but snow boots and shovels were still dry in the closet. Once the snow arrived, the cold took on a whole new meaning. For now, I could enjoy the chilly air and not worry about slipping on ice or scraping my car windshield. The bakery business had slowed since summer, but next week was Thanksgiving, and the pie and dinner roll orders had started coming in. Jack and I would be busy with special orders through New Years. The holidays were the perfect way to fill the void after a busy summer.

"So, this pie contest," Jack started. "They hold it every year?"

"Since I was a kid. The champion back then was the tiniest, frailest woman named Heidi. She made ceramic vases and mugs. People would travel up the mountain just to buy one of her pieces. That was back when the town was still mostly artists and musicians and people who either shunned city life or who couldn't find anyplace else to belong, like my Nana."

Jack had pulled out the ingredients for caramel apple muffins, a sweet, spicy base topped with a brown sugar glaze. They were always a hit at this time of year. "But your Nana is an artist, too," he said.

"Yes, a talent she didn't know she had until she got to town as a young, single mom with nowhere to turn. The townsfolk were like her family. She started to dabble with paints, and the next thing she knew, she was selling her artwork at the weekly craft fair. My mom would sit next to her in the handmade playpen one of the locals built and watch Nana work."

"It must have been wonderful growing up in this town," Jack said.

"It was, even with all the quirky events like the pie eating contest." I rinsed off the mixing bowl and placed it on the drying rack.

Jack set to work peeling apples for the muffins. "That's right. You said a tiny woman was the champion. How many slices of pies did she eat?"

"Actually, that's not how this contest works." I dried off my hands and walked over to the worktable. "Each contestant must eat an entire pie, down to the last crumb of crust, with their hands tied behind their backs."

Jack visualized that for a second and laughed. "So, face-first? Then maybe we should top these with whipped cream."

"Don't worry. That'll happen just before the contest. Each pie gets topped with a mighty mountain of fluffy whipped cream. It's all pretty entertaining. Little Heidi would have her face so deep in cream, she'd nearly disappear. She looked like the kind of woman who would lift her pinky to drink tea and wipe her mouth after each bite of toast, but boy, when it came to that pie contest, she was an animal."

"Does Heidi still compete?" Jack asked.

"She moved to Arizona to be near her daughter and son-in-law. I missed several years of the contest while I was out trying to find my way in the world, but we have a new reigning champion. His name is Emery Gladstone. He owns a nice place a few miles down the mountain." The door opened, and I glanced out to the front of the shop. "And here is his main competitor, Thomas Anderson."

I pulled off my work apron and walked out to greet him. "Thomas, thought you'd be taking a break from baked goods to get ready for the contest."

"I'm here *because* of the contest." Thomas Anderson was a fifty-something man with a round belly and a booming voice. His gray knit beanie had slipped to the side on his mostly bald head, and I badly wanted to right it for him, but he didn't seem to mind it. "I've decided to do a little homework to get ready for the contest. I plan on winning that trophy and the prize money this year." The pie eaters took their competition very seriously. Thomas pulled off his gloves, shoved them in his coat pocket and then stared into the glass case. "Do you have a practice pie?" Now the homework comment was making sense.

"All the pumpkin pies are for the contest, but I have this apple pie. It's the last whole pie I've got."

"Hmm, it's a little different because of the lattice crust on top." He rubbed his chin in thought.

"It'll be a little harder, so maybe that's good because the pumpkin pie will be a breeze in comparison." I found it hard to believe we were having this conversation, but every day was a new adventure in Ripple Creek.

The front door opened and a fresh sweep of crisp, autumn air burst inside, along with Emery Gladstone, Thomas's main competitor and the current champion. The two men glared at each other and then forced friendly smiles. June Greene, Emery's longtime girlfriend, stepped in next. She was huddled in a vanilla white scarf that was piled around her neck like a mound of frosting. Like Emery, June was forty-something. She had refined, pretty features and an elegant way of moving that made her quite the contrast to Emery's heavy, clumsy style. Emery was coarse, like sandpaper, and June was fine, like silk. They were one of those pairs who seemed to confirm the theory that opposites attract.

"Tom, thought you'd be resting up for tomorrow," Emery said snidely. His gaze flashed to the apple pie, the only whole pie in the case. "Scottie, I'd like to buy that apple pie."

Thomas stepped into his line of sight as if physically blocking his access to a pie that was safely tucked behind glass. "Too late. Scottie was just about to box that pie up for me." Thomas's thunderous voice filled the bakery.

Jack heard the angry tones and came out from the kitchen area. He was always sweetly protective.

"Jack, do we have any other whole pies in the back?" I figured the surest way out of this pickle was to produce another pie.

"Only the pumpkin pies for the contest," Jack said.

Thomas looked at me. "I believe I was here first." The truth was he hadn't decided on the apple pie until Emery walked in, but I wasn't going to point that out.

I looked apologetically at Emery. "Maybe you could practice on cake or half a dozen muffins," I suggested.

"It's not the same," Emery said grumpily.

June sighed loudly. "Boy, I wish you took our relationship as seriously as you take this pie contest. But you know what, I'll take one of those chocolate chip cookies, Scottie."

I grabbed a tissue and handed June a cookie. "It's on the house."

"Thanks. This pie contest is ridiculous," she whispered. "Like he's going for an Olympic medal or something."

"Whisper or not, I can hear you," Emery snapped.

"Good. Then you know how I feel." June took a bite of her cookie.

I put together a box for the pie and lifted it out of the case.

"I'll pay you double for that pie," Emery barked.

I smiled politely. "I'm sorry, Emery. Thomas was here first, so he's buying the pie."

Emery huffed a few times and then marched toward the door. "Let's go, June," he grunted.

June stopped at the door. "Delicious cookie, Scottie. Thanks."

I waved as she walked out, then I packed up the pie for Thomas. Thomas was wearing a grin that seemed to indicate, contest or not, he'd just had a fantastic morning.

two
. . .

"I'M GOING over to Roxi's to see if she has some more cinnamon. I can't believe I didn't order enough when we're clearly heading into cinnamon season." I hung up my apron.

"I'll finish these muffins. Should I weigh out flour and salt for next week's bread?" Jack asked.

"That'd be great. I won't be long." I headed to the front door and stopped cold as my gaze landed on the market across the street. Dalton Braddock, the town's ranger and my childhood crush, was leaving the market with his fiancée, Crystal Miramont.

Crystal's family owned the posh resort at the top of the mountain. She was wearing an impractical pair of bright blue high heels and a short fur coat as she clung tightly to Dalton's arm. The two were supposed to get married in a pricey, lavish wedding ceremony this summer, but Dalton called it off. After my own cancelled wedding and major lifestyle shift, I'd finally pulled myself together and settled into a happy existence, but

Dalton threw that into turmoil when he confessed that he'd broken things off with Crystal because he had feelings for me, feelings that started back in middle school. I was stunned, to say the least. I'd spent all of my school years pining for Dalton Braddock, secretly doodling his name on my spiral notebook, peering at him over the edge of my history textbook and falling all over myself with nervous excitement whenever he spoke to me, and all that time he'd liked me, too. I cried rivers when his family packed up and moved out of Ripple Creek. When I'd recently returned to my hometown, I discovered that he'd left his law enforcement position in the city and taken up a position in Ripple Creek. I'd also discovered, much to my dismay, that he was engaged to Crystal Miramont. I grew up with Crystal as well, but we were never friends. It was ironic because she considered the people who lived in the little cottages in Ripple Creek to be beneath her, only I'd come to Ripple Creek as a newly orphaned child with a trust fund that would put the Miramont fortune to shame. Nana and I never told anyone about my money, and I still kept it to myself. I'd had to suffer the tragic loss of both parents to receive that money, so it was hard to even touch it. I had my bakery and my Nana, and I didn't need anything else.

The whole stressful turn of events ended when I couldn't decide how I felt about Dalton leaving Crystal, and Crystal was so distraught that Dalton decided to return to her with the condition that they delay the marriage. Crystal had made it starkly clear that she didn't want me talking to Dalton, and so we'd been keeping our distance. It wasn't easy, though, in a small town.

"Oh, you're still here," Jack said over my shoulder. He glanced out the window and saw the couple as they walked toward the coffee shop. "I see," Jack said quietly. "You're too good for him. And whenever I see those two, he looks as if he wants to chew off the arm that she's holding so tightly."

I snickered.

"Seriously," Jack said.

I patted his arm. "Thanks, Jack."

"Still no word from Cade?" he asked and then rolled in his lips as if he wanted to take the question back. "Sorry, none of my business."

Cade Rafferty had been an essential, albeit unwitting, part of the earlier turmoil. We'd been friends on the cusp of something more for months, and Cade finally kissed me. It coincided with Dalton's declaration of feelings for me. It was a situation that would have sent my teenage self into a state of bliss, but the adult Scottie, not so much. My feelings were so fraught with indecision, I ended up pushing Cade away. He had an offer to go on a European book tour for his latest novel, and so off he went. It was supposed to be for a few weeks, but Cade's personal appearances had improved book sales so much, his publisher pleaded with him to stretch out the tour. I hadn't seen him all summer, and I missed him terribly. My intuition told me our friendship was over, and that made me sadder than seeing Dalton and Crystal strolling around town together.

"It's all right, Jack. I don't mind. Cade's last email said he had no definite date of return. I think he was in France or Italy or something. Anyhow, I'm off for the cinnamon."

The fresh air snapped the touch of melancholy out of my head as I hurried across to Roxi's store. Roxi was standing behind the counter checking out June Greene. I caught snippets of the conversation as I waved to Roxi and headed to the baking aisle. I was in luck—there were two bottles of cinnamon left. I carried them up to the checkout counter where June was still complaining to Roxi about Emery's apparent lack of commitment.

"I mean, I'm not getting any younger," June said. "I told him either I get a ring on this finger"—she pointed out her ring finger—"or we're through."

Roxi's eyes rounded. "You gave him an ultimatum? How did he react?" Roxi was wearing a skeptical brow. I was with her. I'd known a friend in college who gave her longtime boyfriend an ultimatum, the same one June had given Emery, and the boyfriend took the off-ramp and said goodbye.

"Emery told me this wasn't the time to bring up an engagement." June smiled politely at me. "Scottie knows. You heard him this morning. He's so involved with this silly pie eating contest, he says he has to concentrate on that right now. Can you imagine? A pie eating contest."

Roxi held back a laugh. "Maybe you should rethink this whole thing," she suggested.

June nodded once sharply. "That's exactly what I told him. I said if the pie contest is more important than me, then I've been wasting my time with him." Her phone rang. "That's my sister. Just wait until she hears about all this." She picked up her bag of groceries and left the counter.

As June walked out, Regina walked in. She was both Roxi and Nana's friend and the owner of the local gift shop. "Oh, what have I missed? June looked like a woman on a mission." Regina was also the town gossip, which said a lot considering how much gossip floated around town. She glanced at the cinnamon bottles. "That reminds me, I need some cinnamon for my snickerdoodles. It's my great-grandma's recipe, only she was using lard for the fat." Regina scrunched up her nose.

I looked at Roxi. "And that reminds me—I just took your last bottles of cinnamon."

"Well, darn," Regina said.

"I've got some more in the back. I always stock up at this time of year." Roxi looked at me pointedly.

"Yes, as the owner of the local bakery, I should have stocked up, too, but I hadn't planned to bake the pies for the contest."

"Oh, that silly thing," Regina said. "When are they going to get tired of that tradition? So, I saw Dalton and Crystal walking toward the coffee shop." Regina was the master of the dramatic topic switch. "As usual, she was wearing that big, perfectly white smile, and Dalton looked as if he'd rather be anywhere else."

"I'm sure you're misreading that," I said. "Dalton is a grown man. If he was unhappy, he'd break it off."

"Thought he tried that and his bride-to-be threw a hissy fit," Roxi said.

"Yes, but he still went back to her." And as I said the words aloud, they struck a chord, somewhere deep down. He still went back to her. How strong could his feelings be for me if he turned back to Crystal so quickly?

"Scottie?" Regina's voice poked into my thoughts.

"Huh?" I asked.

"I was just asking if Cade had returned?"

"Uh, no, not yet." It was another topic change I could have done without. I was really regretting not ordering enough cinnamon.

"This is much longer than expected, isn't it?" Regina asked with an innocent grin even though she knew the answer.

"It is, Regina."

Roxi stepped in. She was always a good mediator. "Regina,

Scottie already told us that the tour had been extended because his presence was selling a lot of books. Not surprising," Roxi added. "He's such a handsome, charming man."

"I agree," I said, and I meant it. Not having him in my life had left a void. I really missed him. I paid for the cinnamon. "You girls have a nice day. I'll see you later."

"Bye," they said in unison. I didn't need to be the proverbial fly on the wall to know that Regina continued the topic of both Cade and Dalton long after I walked out.

three
...

NANA WAS RAKING leaves in the front yard when I arrived home for lunch. Her long gray braid swung like a pendulum with each stroke of the rake. My grandmother was in her eighties, but she never let a little thing like eight decades slow her down. When people asked her the secret to living such a long, productive life, she always gave them the same answer—don't sit too long on your bottom, and don't take yourself too seriously. A good bowl of soup now and then doesn't hurt either, she always added. And I could smell one of those good bowls of soup as I walked across the yard. She had an impressive pile of brown and gold maple leaves piled up under her sprawling tree.

"I think this is the most leaves this tree has ever dropped," Nana said as she rested the rake against the chalky gray trunk.

"And I think you say that every year. Do I smell broccoli soup?" I asked.

She laughed. "I suppose broccoli is the one vegetable you can count on to announce itself long before you get to the kitchen."

We walked up the front steps. "It did really get a bum rap in the aroma department, but it sure is tasty." I opened the door for her.

Nana was smiling and shaking her head. "You don't know how many years I waited for my little Scottie to say those words—that broccoli was tasty."

"It's an acquired taste, and I think that mostly has to do with the aforementioned topic—it's propensity for being stinky."

We headed to the kitchen. Nana rarely bothered to put away her soup pot at this time of year. We were both big fans of a hot bowl of soup. Her lentil and minestrone were best for taking off the chilly edge of winter. Broccoli and butternut squash soups were the perfect accompaniments to crisp fall afternoons where raking massive piles of leaves and baking pumpkin pies were the orders of the day.

And then there was Nana's tomato soup. Her tomato soup paired with a grilled cheese always took me back to my childhood, or my second childhood, as I called it. My life started much differently, with both my parents highly successful and motivated to have all the luxuries life had to offer. They died in an avalanche while skiing in the Alps. Nana was the complete opposite. Worldly pursuits and material wealth had never interested her. She got joy and satisfaction from experiences and the people around her. After leaving behind a penthouse, a nanny and a cook who'd make all my pancakes in the shapes of animals, I slipped into Nana's simple, wonderful life very easily.

Nana ladled the steaming soup into bowls, and I pulled a box of soda crackers out of the cupboard.

"I invited Dalton," she said.

I dropped the box on the floor. We both stared down at it for a second.

"He said he couldn't make it," Nana continued. "I guess if I'd started with that part, you wouldn't have dropped the crackers."

I picked up the box without comment.

"Don't you want to know why he couldn't make it?" she asked as we both sat down to our lunch.

"Not really. Besides, I already know. He was with Crystal earlier." I opened the crackers and pulled out a stack. I dropped them on top of the hot soup to get them soaked and gooey.

Nana laughed. "Some things never change."

"What?" I looked at the crackers on the surface of the soup. "It's tradition. Broccoli soup gets a cracker coating."

"He said he was very busy with work," Nana continued, even though I was working hard to show little interest in the topic. "He never brought up Crystal."

The soup was hot, so I set down my spoon. "Nana, about inviting Dalton over—"

"He loves my soup. You know that. And this is soup season." Eighty years old also meant eight decades of stubbornness built into one sturdy brick wall.

"Nana, Dalton and Crystal are working on patching things up and having him here—well, it's just counterproductive. Things are much more strained between us, and Crystal made it *crystal* clear that she didn't want me to socialize or hang out or even talk to Dalton."

Nana put her spoon down hard enough in her soup that it splashed. "Now, isn't that ridiculous. Who does she think she is telling you who you can and cannot talk to?"

"I agree, she's ridiculous, but it's just easier if I avoid Dalton, and having him here in our tiny kitchen at our wobbly table makes that hard."

Nana grabbed the edges of the table and gave it a little shake.

"I fixed it by shoving a piece of cardboard under the short leg. Well, I'm not one to get involved in your social life…" She actually said it with a straight face, so I decided not to challenge her on her comically false statement.

A knock was followed by the door opening. Our neighbor, Hannah Redmond, usually gave us the courtesy of a knock before barging in.

"We're in here, Hannah," Nana called.

"Just follow the stink," I said.

Hannah crinkled her nose as she entered the kitchen. "Broccoli soup. I guessed it before I even stepped inside."

Nana started to get up to ladle a bowl for Hannah. "No, sit down, Evie. I already ate." Nana settled back on her chair, and Hannah joined her at the table. Her cheeks were pink from the cold air, and her blue-gray eyes sparkled with what I could only assume was some gossip she had to share. Hannah could definitely give Regina a run for her money, but Regina wouldn't give her crown up easily.

Hannah was wearing a thick, fluffy rust-colored sweater. She pulled it closer around her and shivered once for effect. "Winter is coming. I can feel it in my bones."

"It's on the calendar, too." Nana pointed at the calendar on the fridge.

Hannah waved off her sarcasm. "I just heard from Marge Bivens over on Meadowlark Lane. You know her, I'm sure. She owns a sweet little farmhouse with an acre or so of land. Her place borders a much bigger property owned by a rather disagreeable man named Emery Gladstone." Hannah always felt the need to reacquaint my grandmother with everyone in town even though Nana never forgot a name or a face.

"Emery doesn't seem that disagreeable." I dipped my spoon

into the mush of crackers and soup. My concoction was now perfect for consumption. "He came in to buy a pie for practice before tomorrow's contest."

Hannah didn't like to be contradicted. She pulled her sweater a little tighter and sat up straighter. "Yes, well maybe when he's eating pies, he's more likable. But poor Marge is beside herself. She owns a dozen hens, beautiful birds that lay marvelous eggs. Marge is very fond of her flock. They're like her children, and that's why she's in such a state."

"I don't understand," Nana said. "What do her hens have to do with Emery Gladstone?"

Hannah reached for the cracker box. "Apparently, Emery owns a big dog—"

I put up my hand. "Wait, if this story is going the way I think it is—then maybe it's best to leave out details."

Hannah didn't like being cut short on her storytelling. "It's not as bad as you might think. The dog merely jumped the fence and started chasing the hens around. Gave them a good scare and I imagine there were a few feathers flying, but all the hens are still alive. But they're so shaken up Marge is worried they won't leave the coop for weeks. And this wasn't the first time it happened. She complained to Emery and told him that his fence was too low for such a big dog, but Emery refused to apologize or do anything about it." Hannah sat back with a satisfied grin. "And so, you see—he *is* disagreeable." She sat forward and picked up the box of crackers again. She reached her hand inside and pulled out some pieces. "Why are all these crackers broken?"

Nana arched a brow my direction. "They had a little accident."

"Anyhow, poor Marge is beside herself, and I probably won't hear the end of her hen saga for a few weeks," Hannah said.

"I've never seen her so mad. She told me 'I hope Emery chokes on his pie crust tomorrow. It'll serve him right.' Wait…doesn't Dalton usually come over for soup? Where is he?" Hannah asked.

With all the abrupt topic changes, if I wasn't careful, I was going to end up with whiplash today. I had no response, so I picked up the box of crackers and poured the broken bits into my soup.

four
. . .

I COULD NEVER UNDERSTAND the science behind the Thanksgiving-like fullness that came from a simple bowl of soup. And broccoli soup was especially notorious as a belly filler. I could have easily stretched out on the couch for a nap, but I needed to get back to the bakery. The afternoon had warmed enough that a simple beanie and light coat were all I needed for a bike ride back to the bakery. I hoped the brisk ride would snap me out of my post-soup grogginess.

The sky was a sapphire blue with a few white puffs of cloud. The sun had shifted lower to its seasonal position in the sky, but it was still intense. I pulled down my beanie to cover my ears, adjusted my sunglasses and set off toward town.

As I crossed the bridge and reached the fork in the road that led either to town or to the Gramby Estate, I made a last second decision to turn toward the estate. I'd promised Cade that I'd occasionally stop at the property to check on the house and gardens. The Gramby Estate had been built by Arthur Gramby, a rich mine owner and Cade's great-grandfather. No one had lived in the house for years, and the entire estate had fallen into disrepair. As kids, my friends and I considered it to be the neighborhood's token haunted house. We'd ride our bikes around the old house and hide in the overgrown gardens, jumping out and scaring ourselves silly.

Cade had spent a lot of money bringing the place back to its former glory. He took care to have the gardens restored so that they resembled the old photos he found of the house. Much of the money he'd spent had gone into making sure the structure and foundation were sound and that the roof and windows kept the weather out. There was still plenty to do, but the place looked so much brighter and happier since Cade moved in.

I pedaled up the long, gravel drive to the house, and as the grounds came into view, I spotted a silver SUV parked in front of the house. I pedaled faster and was breathing embarrassingly hard by the time I reached the garden steps. (I blamed it on the soup and crackers.) I rested my bike against the shrubs and hurried up the steps to the upper garden. A man in a dark blue suit and gold tie stepped out from the patio area. He had a gold nametag on his suit, but I couldn't read it from where I stood.

"Excuse me, can I help you?" I asked. "This is private property."

He had a round face, and his hair was slicked down with some kind of greasy product. His smile was broad and flashy. Nana would have called it a "salesman smile," and since he was already pulling out a business card, her assessment would have been right. His silver watch glittered on his thick wrist as he handed me the card.

"How do you do? I'm Charles Willoughby, but you can call me Chuck. I'm a—"

"Realtor," I finished for him. I read the embossed lettering on the card. "Specializing in luxury properties and mountain estates." I took off my sunglasses. "I'm sorry. This property is not for sale. The owner is—"

"In Europe." This time he finished for me. "I know. A book tour. Exciting stuff. I'm a big fan of his work. Mr. Rafferty contacted me and asked me to come by and look at the property, so I could figure out a good price."

His words were striking me like sharp pieces of shrapnel. Cade had decided to sell his Gramby Estate? Chuck kept talking, but the only words going through my head were "Cade no longer wants to live in Ripple Creek. Our friendship is over."

"What did you say your name was?"

"Uh, I didn't. I'm Scottie Ramone. Mr. Rafferty asked me to check on the place occasionally."

Chuck had a wobbly double chin that shook when he nodded. "That's a good idea. You can't be too careful with these lovely old places. Especially one in such a remote, scenic location." His gaze swept across the grounds. "What a magnificent site, too. I have at least a dozen clients who will vie for the first showing. And I think Mr. Rafferty will be pleased with how quickly it'll sell."

I felt my posture deflate with each sentence. Could Cade really be leaving this place? More importantly, could he really be leaving me? And why was my chest aching so much about the whole thing? I would be losing a good friend, of course, but there was more to it. That deep thud in my chest—that was my heart breaking. It was a reaction that I was having a hard time interpreting until it hit me like a ton of bricks. It was Cade. He was the one. I'd had to go out of my way to avoid Dalton for months, and not interacting with him like usual had hurt me and left me feeling as if there was a void in my life, but the notion of Cade leaving Ripple Creek and never looking back felt far worse. I didn't want him to go. I wanted him to be a part of my life. I wanted Cade.

Chuck had been blathering on about something having to do with the maintenance on the house, but my own emotional eruption, as silent as it had been, drowned out his words. Now he stood and waited expectantly, his ample brows doing a questioning dance.

"I'm sorry. It's probably better if you direct all your questions to Mr. Rafferty. Like I said, I'm just a friend"—while my brain silently added *an unimportant and easy-to-leave one at that*—"who promised to check in on the place."

"I understand. Of course." Chuck took a deep breath. His barrel chest strained the buttons on his coat. "Ah, there's nothing like mountain air. Most of my clients will want the place as a vacation home, of course. I'll bet this place is really something covered in glistening snow. And I know the Miramont Resort is just up the hill. Having it so close will put a premium on the price." I was waiting for little dollar signs to appear in his eyes.

"The roads are mostly impassable, and after a big snowstorm, we're the last town to get dug out. The snowplows concentrate on the main mountain roads and the ones around the resort. The owners could be snowed in for several days. And in the summer, we're overrun with tourists. You can hardly take a step in town without tripping on someone's foot or bicycle tire."

My dire descriptions didn't wipe the grin off his face. He chuckled. "I'm sure people interested in the property will research the area and make sure it fits with their idea of a vacation home. Most people looking for a mountain retreat aren't worried about a few feet of snow."

"Rattlesnakes," I blurted. "We've got those, too. And then there was the case of the beheaded statues." I was like a kid trying to convince my parents why summer camp was a bad idea, and the whole act was shamefully bad, but I couldn't stop myself. My last detail had caught his attention.

His thick brows rustled together. "Beheaded statues?" He glanced around at the landscape. "I don't see any statues."

"That's because each and every one of them had their heads chopped off." I drew my finger across my throat for an unnecessary visual. "Never caught the culprit." Now I was even resorting to lies. It was amazing how easily the threat of a broken heart could turn you into a semi-hysterical lunatic.

Chuck smiled politely. "Well, I suppose since there are no more statues in the yard, we won't have to worry about it anymore."

The phrase "haunted and rife with unhappy poltergeists" was at the tip of my tongue, but I told myself that the nutty banana show needed to stop. Cade wanted to sell the Gramby Estate, and it was his right to do so. Obviously, there was nothing I could do to change that.

Chuck's phone rang. For a moment, I wondered if it was Cade. I had to resist the urge to pull the phone from Chuck's stubby fingers and plead with Cade not to sell. But since he promised the person on the other end that he'd stop for milk and eggs on his way home, it saved me the dramatic moment and the opportunity to embarrass myself more.

"It was nice meeting you, Ms. Ramone. And thanks for taking care of the place." He got in his car, and I trudged down the steps to my bike. I looked back at the house. It didn't look all that happy and bright, after all.

five
. . .

I PEDALED over the bridge and took the fork toward town. My mind was so splattered with thoughts of Cade leaving, and my chest was so heavy with the notion that I was losing him, that I hardly paid attention to the traffic. Never a good idea on a bicycle. I'd allowed my bike to venture too far into the road. The truck honked as it roared past me. It was dragging a long trailer that bounced and shimmied on the hard asphalt. I turned my handlebars sharply in reaction. After a few seconds of trying to correct my front wheel, I wobbled but regained my balance. "Jerk!" I yelled at the truck driver, even though I was more at fault. I recognized the green paint on the truck. It belonged to Gladstone and Hermann Excavation. Emery Gladstone and his partner, Doug Hermann, had a small fleet of large machinery for excavation of construction sites.

I stopped and put my feet down to collect myself. My heart was still racing. I needed to pull myself together. Cade had made his decision, and there wasn't anything I could do about it.

After I broke off the engagement with Jonathan Rathbone, I told myself I'd never let a man get in the way of my life or future again. Now, here I was, dazed and confused and stunned about Cade's decision to leave Ripple Creek. Cade had kissed me, and instead of telling him right then that I wanted to pursue a relationship, I acted like a dithering fool. That was Dalton's fault. My emotions were so scrambled, I couldn't figure out what I wanted. Now I knew, and it was too late. I'd finally come to a solid conclusion, but now it didn't matter because Cade had moved on and made other plans.

I looked cautiously behind me and put my feet back on the pedals. The massive truck and trailer were long gone, and the road was quiet. I rode to the bakery, locked up my bike and went inside. The soup had filled me, but suddenly, a large fudge brownie seemed in order. I was in luck. There were still a few in the case. I hadn't flipped over the sign that we were back from lunch yet. I needed a minute with my thoughts and my brownie. There was still some coffee in the pot. I poured it into a cup and zapped it in the microwave. I sat down with the brownie and immediately took a bite.

The front door opened. Jack was back from lunch, too. He was talking to someone as he entered. I figured he was on a phone call, but when he walked back to the kitchen, he looked at me and then at the brownie and then back at me. Jack and I had grown quite close in a short time, and he had a great intuition about everything and life in general.

"You have a visitor, but something tells me you'd rather stay here with the brownie. I guess I'm going to need to hear more about your lunch, but first, should I tell him you're busy?"

"Who is it?"

"Oh, I thought you heard us talking. It's Dalton."

I stared down at the half-eaten brownie. Dalton was probably the last person I needed to see. "That's okay." I took another big bite and nodded approvingly as I chewed and swallowed. "We are brilliant bakers." Normally, if I heard that Dalton was in the shop, my resident butterflies would do a little dance, and there'd be the slightest tremble in my knees, but that didn't happen. My crush on Dalton would always be a big part of my life, a big part of me, but it seemed I'd finally managed to get past it.

All of this was happening so fast. I blamed it on the shock of finding out that Cade was leaving. Was that it? I asked myself as I left the kitchen. Was I suddenly pining for Cade only because he was leaving? Was his unexpected change in plans the reason for my new feelings? Ugh, so many confusing thoughts. I tamped them down and pushed up a faint smile. Dalton and I had had only a few conversations in the past few weeks, and our chats always felt strained and awkward. It seemed this conversation wasn't going to be any different. I wasn't sure we'd ever go back to our old selves.

"Are you here for dessert?" I asked. "There are still a few more brownies."

Dalton was shaking his head before I finished. "No, I'm not here for dessert. I just wanted to apologize for not coming for soup."

"Uh, I think you're talking to the wrong person. Nana invited you for soup, not me." I had no idea why I was talking so harshly. And he was taken aback by it.

"Right. Sorry. I guess I'll give Evie a call. I was busy. But I always love her soup. I guess I'll head out."

"No, wait, I'm sorry Dalton. It's just been a—" If there was one person I had no intention of telling about Cade moving and my subsequent heartbreak, it was Dalton. The two men had disliked each other from the start. And as much as Nana had tried to convince me that their mutual dislike had to do with me, I'd scoffed at the notion. But now, it seemed Nana had been right all along. Not surprising. Nana was rarely wrong.

Dalton looked confused about whether he should stay or not.

I lifted a finger. "Just a second." I walked to the back. "Jack, I'm going to step out for a minute."

"No problem. I'll keep an eye on the shopfront."

I hurried back out and half-expected Dalton to have left, but he was still there with a lost expression, one that I'd seen on him before. I had no idea if it was the emotional shock from earlier or if all my new feelings had settled into a nice neat pile in my brain, but I had an urge to clear the air between us…hopefully, for good.

"Come with me," I said, and Dalton followed without question. There was a bench just past Esme's bookstore. I sat down, and Dalton sat next to me.

"What's going on?" he asked.

"First of all, let me just say that I hate this new thing between us. We're like two strangers half the time, strangers who are entirely too familiar to actually be strangers." I shook my head. "That came out monstrously wrong."

"No, I get it, and I agree. We know each other too well to act so coldly and distant when we're together. Look, Scottie, Crystal and I—" He rubbed his forehead. "We're fighting a losing battle. The therapy, the romantic dinners, spending what she considers quality time together—none of it is bringing us closer. We're from different worlds and always will be. I'm far more suited to someone who rides her bicycle to her bakery and goes home to eat soup with her grandmother at lunch."

I tamped down a smile. (If he only knew my net worth.) "Dalton, if you knew how often my thirteen-year-old-self longed to hear those words from you—well—you'd—you'd—" I laughed. "You'd probably run for the hills. I was that crazy about you."

Dalton rested back with a chuckle. "And I was a thick-headed kid who was so tuned into my skateboard and video games, I had no clue. But I did like you, always. I used to love it whenever the teacher asked the two of us to stay after and clean paintbrushes or chalkboards. It gave me time alone with you, and you were always funny and sweet and incredible." His expression saddened. "But? I get the feeling there was a big 'but' coming." We both took a second to laugh about what he'd said, proving there was still a touch of kid in both of us.

"*But,*" I continued after our burst of laughter. "I realized recently—" (like a half hour ago) "—that I've finally let go of those crazy, intense feelings I had for you." I hadn't expected such a profound reaction on his face. "Don't get me wrong, there will always be this niche carved out of my heart just for Dalton Braddock. Always." Now that I'd started this, I decided to lay it all out there. "You were my first and longest crush. You hold that distinction and no one else ever will." I took hold of his hand, and our gazes locked. How often I'd dreamt about gazing dreamily into those brown eyes, and they did not disappoint. Ever. "I desperately want to remain friends, and I hope that someday that will be the case."

Dalton looked away for a second. "Crystal tries to control too much of my life. She's always gotten her way, and I think she's holding on to the idea of us only because she sees it as a piece of her life where she isn't getting her way."

"Your relationship with Crystal is your own business, and I

would never give any advice on it, but I will tell you this, Dalton, you need to listen to what your heart is telling you."

I let go of his hand.

"I'm going to. I'm done with this dance the two of us have been in for the past few months. I'm not happy. I haven't been happy." He turned toward me. "I may never forgive my thirteen-year-old self for being such a thick-headed dimwit."

I laughed. "Hey, go easy. That's my crush you're talking about. By the way—in case you're wondering—the name 'Scottie Ramone Braddock' looks beautiful in purple marker, and I think my math notebook had it in green."

He arched a brow. "Ramone Braddock?"

"You can't expect me to give up a cool last name like Ramone."

"I guess not." He sighed. "Thanks, Scottie. I think this talk helped in a lot of ways. It doesn't lift the lead in my chest, but I think it'll help me move on with my life." He glanced around and then leaned over and kissed my cheek. Some of those butterflies woke up, but they were definitely less energetic now.

six
...

JACK HAD the mixer running in the back, whipping up vanilla bean frosting for cupcakes. Esme, my friend and the owner of the Nine Lives Bookshop next door, walked in seconds after I entered the bakery.

"What was going on out there?" she asked excitedly. Of course, Esme knew all about my past and present feelings for Dalton, and she knew I was in a state of confusion about Cade. "I saw you two having a heart-to-heart." Her hand flew to her mouth. "Oh my gosh, has Regina rubbed off on me? Suddenly, I'm a nosy gossip." She shook her head emphatically. "You don't have to tell me anything. None of my business." She started backing up. "I'll go back to the store. I have some shelves to dust."

"Esme, stop right there. You're not being nosy because you're my friend, and since I've already bored you with all my tales of romance woes, I should at least provide you with an ending."

Esme perked up. She was wearing one of her signature bookseller aprons. This one was adorned with little turkeys and fall leaves for the upcoming holiday. She clapped quickly. "Yay, I love a brilliant happy ending." She paused and looked at me. "Oh no, not a happy ending?"

"Is it that obvious? I told Dalton he needs to move on with his life, whether that's with Crystal or not. It's not going to be with me."

Esme's eyes rounded. "So, it's Cade." She smiled smugly. "I knew it. I had a bet with myself that it was going to be Cade. I do adore him. Naturally, as a bookseller, I'm partial to writers. Plus, there's just something about him..." She finally paused her long speech and looked at me again. "Oh boy, I just keep stepping in it."

I laughed and hugged her. "It's all right. You've been stuck listening to this soap opera for so long, I'm sure you were hoping for a satisfying conclusion so you wouldn't have to hear about it anymore."

"Not true. Since my own love life is at the ground level—check that—basement level, it's nice to hear what's happening in your love life. What's going on? Is Cade not coming home soon? Does he know that you chose him? And now I'll pull the zipper shut so you can talk." She pulled the invisible zipper across her lips.

"I have no idea when Cade is coming home, and no, I haven't told him, and I probably won't because—circumstances have changed."

Esme twisted her mouth in confusion. She pointed to her lips.

"Permission to pelt me with more questions," I said with a laugh.

"Does that mean you've decided to be with Dalton? I knew it.

I had a bet with myself that you'd end up with Dalton."

"Didn't you just say you had a bet with yourself that I'd end up with Cade?"

Esme shrugged. "That's why I like betting with myself. I never lose. So, what are the circumstances?"

"Keep this to yourself, but it seems Cade is planning to sell the Gramby Estate. He's leaving Ripple Creek."

Esme's posture deflated. "I hate that ending. Why would he leave?"

"I guess he's not happy here."

"You can change his mind," she offered with a hesitant smile.

"I doubt it." Two customers came in, and I was somewhat thankful. The conversation had left me feeling glum. It wasn't Esme's fault, but saying the whole thing out loud really hit me.

Esme winked. "We'll talk later. And chin up. I think this can still work itself out into a happily ever after."

The rest of the afternoon went slowly. The pies were ready for the contest, and Jack planned to get to the shop early for them to be picked up. I let Jack know a few of the details of my stressful day, but I decided it wasn't my place to spread the word that Cade was moving. Word would get around soon enough when his place went on the market. I briefly wondered if I should buy the estate. I'd been thinking about moving out of Nana's house to give her back her space. I was sleeping in the room where she kept her art supplies. Her house was small, and she liked her hobbies. Besides that, she was a master collector of *stuff*. My presence had put a dent in her collector hobby. Still, I knew she loved having me home, and I loved being there. It would be hard to see the Gramby Estate become a vacation rental. Or what if some truly unlikable people moved in? As much as I'd been thinking about buying my own place, I certainly didn't need an estate or massive house. Apparently, neither did Cade.

The sun was getting lower in the sky, and the temperature had dropped to what I called ear-ache cold. I pulled my beanie down low to cover my ears, but they still throbbed from the brisk air. The bike ride had seemed like a good idea in the warmth of the day, but now I wished I'd driven into town. My hands were numb as I gripped the handlebars. This afternoon's close brush with the massive truck and trailer was still fresh enough in my mind to make me extra cautious.

I crossed the bridge, and, for no apparent reason, I rode toward the Gramby Estate. Was I still thinking about buying it? I cleared that notion from my head. I couldn't imagine wandering the long hallways of the house without Cade. It would only remind me what a fool I was to hesitate after our kiss.

I rode toward the estate with a low thump in my chest. I missed hanging out there with Cade. I missed our coffee chats where we'd spend so much time laughing that our coffees would turn cold and undrinkable. I missed our late evening dinners where we toasted to ridiculous things like the best brand of boxed mac and cheese or a lack of mosquitoes in the garden.

The sun was setting faster, and the shadows stretched long over the landscape. The house always looked commanding as it peered out over the gardens, especially on a cold autumn night. Much of the early fall color was gone, and the trees were starting to grow long skeletal arms. I parked the bike. I wouldn't stay long.

I tugged down the edges of the beanie, but it wasn't doing much to block the cold from my ears. I'd left the house without gloves, so my fingers were numb. I shoved my hands into my coat pockets and climbed the steps to the house. I knew something was off almost instantly. A window was open on the bottom floor. Something clanged inside.

I raced to the side with the open window and ducked down beneath it. Another clang. Darkness was starting to march its way across the lot, making the unexplained noises seem louder. It wasn't helping my courage level either. I was apparently not a great house sitter. It seemed someone had entered the house and was now causing havoc inside. The first thing that usually came to mind in a situation like this was a phone call to the police; however, that meant Dalton would show up to the house. I didn't feel like explaining why I was at Cade's place. I wasn't exactly sure myself.

I took a deep breath and straightened enough to look through the window. I couldn't see anyone, but a light was on. It seemed to be coming from the kitchen. I crept out from below the window and took another deep breath as I headed to the side door leading to a mudroom and the kitchen. Night was falling much faster than I anticipated. Each day grew shorter, but today the sunlight seemed to have shut down early. I moved stealthily along the rough stone wall and managed to hook my foot on a wound-up garden hose. I gasped as I fell forward and couldn't stop myself from crying out as my knees hit the gravelly ground.

Footsteps grew louder, and the side door flew open before I could push to my feet. A tall shadow loomed over me. I lifted my face and peered up at him.

"Ramone? What the heck are you doing down there?" Cade asked. I was so relieved and happy to see him that a whimper slipped out.

"I was checking on the house for you." He offered his hand

and pulled me to my feet. He tugged hard enough that I fell slightly forward. We were only inches apart. I forced a smile. "Looks like everything is in order."

Cade smiled back. "It's good to see you, Ramone."

"It's good to see you, too."

seven
. . .

"YOU'RE LIMPING," Cade said.

"Don't worry. I won't sue even though I was out there skulking around in the dark working to protect your home from intruders." I stopped in the middle of the kitchen and put my hands on my hips. "Seriously, a phone call or text would have been nice. I saw the open window and heard clanging. I thought someone had broken into your house."

Cade waved toward the pot on the stove. "Someone broke in and immediately started clanging pots and pans in the kitchen."

I half-shrugged. "Maybe a hungry thief? And you're avoiding my earlier scolding because you know I'm right. You should have called. Unless, of course…" I let the thought die off.

Cade stepped toward me. He was wearing a dark blue sweater that worked well with his light hazel gaze. His hair was slightly longer, and there was a light shadow of stubble on his chiseled jaw. "'Unless, of course' what?" he prodded. The way he looked at me caused my sore knees to tremble.

I yanked my beanie off, deciding it wasn't the best look for making a serious point. "Unless, of course, you didn't call because you didn't want to talk to me."

Without warning, he reached up and smoothed back the few hairs that had gone wild after I pulled off the knit beanie. His fingertips left a warm trail on my cheek. "How could I not want to talk to my favorite person?"

"You left me for a long time. How *favorite* could I be?"

"You know why I left, Ramone, and it had very little to do with my novel." The turn in conversation thrilled me and made my heart do a few sputters, then my head took over.

"But you're planning on leaving me for good. And don't deny it. I met your realtor. He was practically salivating at the thought of selling this place. And to who? Some rich scoundrel who'll turn it into a vacation rental, then a group of college kids will rent it for the summer and cause all kinds of chaos and shenanigans in the neighborhood."

"Ramone," he said gently. Too gently to stop my tirade.

"Not to mention those lovely gardens you worked so hard to bring back. Or someone will come in and cement the whole place over so that it's all parking spots and driveway. I've seen people do that so they have places to park their fancy cars."

"Ramone," he said again.

"It's not fair that you got me used to this—to us—and then you're just going to pack up your sweaters and your loafers and your computer—"

"Scottie," he said sharply enough to finally help me turn off the spigot.

I blinked up at him. "Well? What do you have to say for yourself, Mr. Rafferty?"

"First, I think we need to sit with a glass of wine. Why don't you wash the grit from your hands, and I'll meet you at the table."

Cade's calm demeanor only made me feel worse about my little scene. It also made me think he didn't care nearly as much about our friendship. He obviously wasn't feeling the same emotional turmoil as me.

I walked to the sink and washed my hands. A cork popped from wine behind me. I turned around and headed to the table as Cade was filling two glasses. There was a small black box sitting at my usual spot at the table. I looked up at him.

"I found it in a shop in Austria and thought of you."

I sat down, not taking my eyes off the box. He'd brought me a gift. Why was he leaving if he brought me a gift? A gift would only make this harder.

"I promise I bought you more than the box. If you open it, there's something inside." He placed the glass of wine in front of me and pulled out a chair.

I lifted the top. A gold charm in the shape of a cupcake and encrusted with tiny diamonds sat in the middle of green velvet lining. I lifted it out. The thin gold chain sparkled nearly as much as the diamonds.

"Cade, it's beautiful and whimsical and sweet." I smiled at him. "I love it." I unfastened the clasp and held the two open ends for him to take. I stood up, and he stood right behind me. The familiar scent of his soap and cologne wafted past me. I'd missed that scent so much.

His warm knuckles grazed the back of my neck as he fastened the clasp. I glanced down at the gold charm. "It's perfect," I said. I turned to him. "Is this so I can think of you after you're gone?" I was still too hurt and confused about his decision to leave Ripple Creek to let a beautiful gift unruffle my feathers.

"Sit," he commanded. I wasn't great at taking commands, but I sat with a plunk. "It's true. While I was away, I had a lot of time to think. Europe, with its charming old towns, cobblestone streets and outdoor cafes, provides a nice backdrop for some heavy soul searching."

Something heartbreaking occurred to me as he spoke. He'd met someone else. I let him go off to Europe thinking I wasn't planning to take our relationship further, so he opened his horizons and met someone else. Most likely a slim, fashionable French woman named Genevieve who wears plum-colored lipstick and eats champagne-soaked strawberries for breakfast.

Cade reached over and took my hand. "I don't want to be friends, Ramone." His gesture of taking my hand didn't line up well with the words, and the words felt like shards of glass.

"You don't?" I was holding back tears.

He shook his head. "I want more than that. But if you're not interested, then I think it's best if I move on. I know one thing for certain, I can't remain here in Ripple Creek if you and Braddock are a couple. It would be like a stake through my already broken heart."

I couldn't hold back a smile, but it was badly timed.

Cade sat back as if I'd slapped him. "Didn't know my broken heart would be so amusing."

"It's not. Especially because my own heart broke in two when Chuck Willoughby announced that you were selling Gramby. I couldn't believe you'd leave me." This time I took his hand. "I don't want to be friends either, Cade."

He seemed to be assessing just what that meant, so I clarified.

"I want more than that," I said.

His hazel eyes glittered. "You mean?"

I nodded. "Yes, I've missed you terribly, and I think you should dump Genevieve and her plum-colored lipstick and French perfume and settle for little old me."

His dark brows bunched. "You've lost me. Who is Genevieve?"

I waved it off. "She's no longer important. What matters is that we both want the same thing."

Cade squinted an eye at me. "So, Braddock?"

"I told Dalton he needed to move on with his life and that we would remain friends, but that was all."

Cade stared at me a long moment. "So, I'm no longer in competition with the ranger?"

"No. What do you think? Can we make this work?"

I was still holding his hand. He didn't answer at first. I looked at him in question.

"I'm thinking," he said. "Chuck said I could get a million and a half for this place."

I tugged to get my hand free. He laughed and pulled me into his lap. "I guess we could make this work." I turned my face to his and we kissed.

eight
. . .

IT WAS dark by the time I got home. Nana was on the front stoop, wringing her hands in worry, and I immediately suffered a pang of guilt for not texting or calling that I'd be late. I supposed I was too giddy to be responsible. After months of turmoil, confusion and an unrelenting ache in my chest, I'd finally landed in the center of what I hoped was the start of my happy ending.

"There you are, and I have a good mind to send you to bed without supper," Nana said sternly. But as I reached the stoop, she pulled me into a hug. She felt frailer in my arms with each hug, but I knew beneath her heavy knit cloak she was still as strong as ever.

I took hold of her thin arms and leaned back to look at her. "I'm so sorry, but I have some news, and that should help. Unless you're really going to send me to bed without supper?"

She took my hand with a laugh. "Come inside. I could do with a nice story. It's been a boring day. Nothing interesting in town and nothing intriguing on the news." I followed her inside. "I've made some macaroni and cheese."

"That should hit the spot after a cold bike ride home." I noticed a cookie tin was sitting on the counter. The familiar, nostalgia-inspiring aroma of her oatmeal cookies floated around it. "You baked cookies?" I asked.

Nana rolled her long braid into a knotted bun at the back of her neck. "Why? Do you think you're the only person in town who can bake a decent cookie?" She turned quickly away from my scrutinizing gaze.

"Get yourself a drink. I've got some fresh iced tea in the refrigerator." Nana spooned some macaroni and cheese onto a plate.

"You're avoiding the cookie topic. Who did you bake for? Or should I ask?" I said curtly.

Nana turned to the table with the plates. She used the macaroni and cheese like a shield. "Now don't be mad—"

"You didn't," I said.

Nana's head tilted slightly to the side, and she added a puppy dog frown to go with it. "I went to the market to get some milk, and I saw Dalton. He was leaving the market with a ready-made sandwich." She made it sound tragic that he was reduced to eating a ready-made sandwich, but Regina's sandwiches were made fresh daily, and they were always delicious. "He looked so sad," she continued. "I invited him for dinner, but he said he wouldn't be able to make it."

The tension in my shoulders released. "Good. You should have led with that." As I said it, there was a knock at the door.

Nana forced a smile that balled up her cheeks. "He's just dropping by for the cookies. When I asked him what was wrong —he told me he wished he could jump back in time and be sitting at our kitchen table eating warm oatmeal cookies and drinking cold milk. He said that was the kind of week he'd been having." She picked up the cookie tin and hurried to the door.

I could hear them talking in the doorway. "This is so sweet of you, Evie. I'm feeling better already just seeing your gorgeous smile and smelling these delicious cookies. I won't even bother with dinner tonight. Going straight to the cookies."

It seemed weird for me to not get up and at least say hello. We'd had our chat, after all, and we were supposed to be on the other side of the awkwardness road. I got up from the table. Dalton's gaze flashed my direction. He smiled shyly. Apparently, we weren't all the way across the road yet. I decided to lighten the mood.

"So, I see you've found a new baker." I looked pointedly at the tin in his hand.

He lifted the cookies and, for a second, he was young Dalton Braddock, standing in my doorway, thanking my grandmother for some cookies. How my heart would race every time he came to the house. "They're Evie's oatmeal cookies," he reminded me.

I nodded. "All right, I admit defeat only because I know they're the best oatmeal cookies this side of the Rockies." Those same oatmeal cookies had gotten me through many tear sessions, and many of them were centered around Dalton Braddock.

"Well, I'll let you two eat dinner." Dalton nodded politely.

"Sure you can't stay?" Nana asked. I really needed to debrief my grandmother on the events of the day.

"No, no. I've got paperwork to do at the office. These cookies will make the task much more enjoyable."

Headlights swept through the window and across the front room. Dalton turned in the doorway to see who'd come up our small street. He turned back and focused solely on me. "Did you know he was back?" I didn't think he'd meant to sound accusatory, but it sure came out that way.

Nana leaned to look past Dalton's broad shoulders. "Who is it? Oh. It's Cade," she said softly. She turned back to me, and while I hadn't told her anything about my day, the pieces seemed to be coming together for her.

"Thanks for the cookies, Evie," Dalton said briskly. He tromped down the steps.

I went to the doorway, excited to see Cade but also badly wishing the whole scene in the front yard was entirely different. Cade climbed out of the car. Both men stared at each other in a silent game of chicken.

"Oh dear," Nana said from behind me.

"Oh dear, indeed," I muttered. I waved enthusiastically to Cade and was devasted when he didn't wave back. He got back in the car. Dalton spun his truck around first. He drove slowly past Cade's car and then smacked down the gas pedal. Cade turned his car around and that was it. The street was empty.

Nana peered up at me. "Did I cause that?"

"You weren't the direct cause. Your cookies were the main culprits."

"Does the story you were going to tell me over dinner have to do with both men?"

"It sure does, only it seems there's been a plot twist." I couldn't help but feel entirely deflated.

Nana took my hand. "Oh, Button, I'm sorry. I didn't mean to cause trouble. Come to the kitchen and tell me all about it. I'm sure we can straighten this out."

By the time we reached the kitchen, I had a new emotion coursing through me—anger. Cade had turned around without waiting for an explanation. I pulled out my phone and sent off a text. "Seriously?? Nana baked Dalton cookies. It had nothing to do with me, but if that's how quickly you change your mind, then I'm not sure this is going to work. I need someone more solid." My fingers were flying, but I stopped to stare at the text for a long moment. Then I tapped send.

I'd been so hungry, and Nana's mac and cheese was always a slice of heaven on my plate, but my appetite had diminished.

Nana sat down across from me. "Button? Aren't you going to eat?"

I stared down at the plate of cheesy noodles.

Nana's chair scraped the floor. She picked up my plate, covered it in plastic wrap and placed it in the refrigerator. Then she plucked up her kitten-shaped cookie jar and carried it over to the table. The aroma of cinnamon-laced oatmeal cookies tickled my nose and sent me back in time.

I lifted the cat head off the jar and reached in for one of the cookies.

"I'll get the milk," Nana said. "Then you can tell me all about it, and your Nana will figure out how to fix it."

I shook my head. "There's no solution, so let's just eat cookies." I glanced at my phone. Cade hadn't texted back. Maybe that was it. He was probably talking to the realtor asking how fast he could sell Gramby Estate, so he could get the heck out of town.

nine
...

SOMETIMES ALL IT took was a new day with a bright sun to snap you out of a funk. But as I got ready to go into town, I was feeling anything but funk-less. A slice of peanut butter and banana toast sat on the table next to a cup of steaming coffee. Nana was trying to make up for last night's debacle with one of my favorite breakfast treats. None of it should have ended with such drama, and I was still sore at Cade over his reaction. He never responded to my text, and I wondered if I, too, had started too much drama with my hastily written message. I broke the big rule of texting. Never dash one off when you're upset or angry. Maybe it was better that Cade hadn't responded. I was sure his reply would have been as full of fire as mine and then we'd be in a full-on feud.

I could hear the tinny sound of the metal rake plowing through crunchy leaves outside the back door. Nana had moved her fall leaf collection to the backyard. Her cup and cereal bowl were in the sink. She got up early but let me sleep late. Jack was manning the bakery this morning, and we closed early on Sunday. It gave us time to get ready for the next week. This morning, we would close early before the pie contest. Most everyone would be gathered at Green Lake Park for the event.

After my cookie dinner, I was hungry. I gobbled down the peanut butter toast (although gobbling peanut butter-covered anything was always slow) and drank the cup of coffee. I had no plans to take my bicycle out, even if the sun was shining. After my late ride, I concluded the cold snap in the air was leaning much more toward winter than fall. The icy months were just a few weeks away, and soon, I'd be digging my car out of snow and clutching the wheel to avoid a spin out on ice.

The back door opened. Nana's cheeks were rosy from the cold and from the raking. "Button, you found the treat. I didn't want to wake you. You're always up so early for work, I figured you could use the sleep."

"Thanks for that, Nana. And the peanut butter toast hit the spot. Are you coming to the pie contest?"

"Oh, that silly thing? No, couldn't be bothered. Dress warmly. It's cold out there this morning. Looks like we'll have winter soon."

"I was thinking the same thing." I carried my plate and cup to the sink and walked over to kiss her cheek. "I'll be home early today, and I look forward to just hanging out. See you later."

People were huddled in winter gear for the brisk walk to the park. It was easier than trying to find a parking spot near the contest. I parked in front of the bakery and went inside. Jack was finishing measuring out balls of bread dough. The dough would go into the refrigerator where they'd develop a nice, complex flavor before being baked on Tuesday when we reopened.

Jack wiped his hands off on his apron. "You look as if you

need a cup of coffee."

"That bad, eh? Actually, it's even worse because I already had a cup of coffee. I see the pies are gone."

"Yep, a woman named Ingrid with a lot of shellac on her hair and a gray suit came in to collect them. She gave me a check. I put it on your desk."

"Thanks. I sold them to the city council at cost since it was a community event. Ingrid Engalls is on the city council. She's in charge of the pie contest. Did the big boxes work? I wasn't sure if there'd be room in her back seat."

"She borrowed her husband's truck, and we put the boxes in back for the short trip to the park." Jack untied his apron. "The country bread loaves are ready for Tuesday. I can measure out the other ingredients after the contest." He paused. "If that's all right. I've always wanted to watch a pie eating contest, and this one seems extra fun. Ingrid said she bought cans of whipped cream to make the whole thing extra messy."

"Of course you can go. I was hoping we'd walk down together."

Jack pulled on his coat, and we headed to the park. "Seems like the whole town showed up for the contest," Jack noted.

"Not sure why, but this pie contest has taken on mythical-like status in the past few years. People post pictures online, and it brings spectators from up and down the mountain." It did seem most of the town was there. I was more interested in the people who *weren't* there. I was fairly certain a pie eating contest was not enough to lure Cade out of his big, stately home. I'd been holding out hope he'd show up, so we could chat. I figured a whipped cream-covered pie eating contest would be a nice, light backdrop for our discussion. Dalton's ranger truck was parked at the park entrance, but I couldn't see him.

A Pie For A Pie

The contest would be held in the gravelly parking lot. The main attraction at Green Lake Park were the chess tables at the shady end of the park. Occasionally, the local chess players would bundle up and endure the cold for a few games of chess, but most of the regulars had forsaken their chess tables for the pie contest. The other attraction at our humble park was the nice walking path that circled the lake. It was really more of a pond, an algae-stricken one at that, but the local ducks didn't seem to mind the size or the slimy bottom. A stroll around the lake was always a nice way to unwind from a stressful day.

Several long tables had been placed end-to-end resulting in a table long enough for sixteen pies and their respective eaters. Names had been written in black felt marker on tented cardboard. Emery would be at the start, or head, of the long table because he was last year's champion. Thomas Anderson's nameplate was in front of the next pie over. Our beautiful from-scratch pies had been topped with tall mounds of manufactured, oil-based whipping cream. Contestants were already being fitted with plastic aprons. I didn't see Emery or Thomas at the table. I expected to see June Greene, Emery's longtime girlfriend, standing up front, getting ready to cheer him on, but I didn't see her anywhere.

Dalton's tall head appeared in the crowd and seeing him brought back the unfortunate ending to my evening. It seemed as if the contest was still a few minutes off. "You know, Jack, I think I'll take a brisk walk around the lake."

"Everything all right?" he asked. "You didn't seem yourself when you walked in this morning."

I sighed loudly. "Only a few cracks in an otherwise perfect existence, Jack."

Jack glanced across to Dalton. He was talking to Ingrid

Engalls. "Would those cracks both be over six feet tall?"

"They would." I winked. "See you in a few." I pointed down at the small space around me. "Hold my place. This park is getting crowded."

I headed toward the walking trail. The shrubs and tall grasses that lined the path all spring and summer had shrunk back to spindly nests of bare branches. I turned the first corner and spotted Emery walking briskly in my direction. He looked as if he was in a sort of meditative state, like a major athlete before a game.

He spotted me and smiled. "Can't wait to dive face-first into one of your pies," he said with a chortle.

"They're much better with a fork, but I guess to each his own. I didn't think I'd see you out here on the path. Thought you'd be up at the table getting ready for the contest."

"I always come out here and do a brisk walk to clear my head and work up the appetite for that pie."

I spotted someone coming up behind him on the path. It was Thomas. Emery noticed me looking past his shoulder and turned back. "And Thomas has decided to copy me this year," he said sharply.

Thomas was wearing a friendly grin as he reached us. "Last I heard, this was a public park, and anyone was welcome to walk the path."

"You're copying me and trying to steal all my training ideas," Emery said.

It was hard to keep from laughing. The two were treating this like a sport.

"I hardly think a walk around the park will go down as a legendary training technique," Thomas quipped. "Besides, walk or not, I intend to win this year." He bowed politely to me. "Miss

Ramone. Thank you for baking the delicious pies. I think I'll head to the contest and get suited up for this." He grinned at Emery. "It's going to be a massacre." With that, he sauntered away with jaunty steps and that same big grin.

"I don't know about that guy," Emery said. "I think he's up to something. I think he's planning to cheat."

I turned back to Emery. "How on earth can he do that? There's going to be well over a hundred people watching you eat your pies."

Emery shook his head. "I don't know what he's got planned, but I don't trust him."

"Well, good luck, and I hope the best pie eater wins." I hurried off. The last thing I wanted was to get involved in a pie eating contest controversy. I had my own controversies to deal with.

ten
. . .

THE ENERGY in the crowd was growing as the contestants stood behind their chairs in their plastic aprons. Ingrid and her assistant, Diedre, a young woman who spent a lot of time studying in the bookshop, tied the contestants' hands behind their backs. They waited for the cue to sit. Ingrid was standing in her prim gray suit with straight posture as if she was about to oversee something very important.

Jack leaned sideways. "This sure is a big deal."

"I told you—it's taken on a life of its own in the past few years. Social media," I added. "Honestly, I think Ingrid is dragging this out because there are so many people, and she wants to make it worth their while."

"I see, so she's building up the suspense, eh?" Jack asked.

I chuckled. "Something like that. The actual pie-eating portion of the contest doesn't take all that long."

"Definitely not as long as it took us to bake those pies." Jack stretched up to get a better look at the table. "Seems a shame to

A Pie For A Pie

pile that fake whipped cream on those pies, but I suppose the cream gives the whole contest a little more pizazz."

"It sure does." I hated that my gaze always managed to find Dalton in a crowd. As far as I knew, he hadn't seen me, and I was good with that. He walked across to his truck; his phone pressed to his ear. He got in the truck and pulled out of the parking lot.

"Seems like the ranger isn't sticking around for the fun," Jack noted.

"I'm sure Crystal called him up to the resort for some minor crime. She calls him for fender benders in the resort parking lot." I wasn't exaggerating. Crystal and the whole Miramont family treated Ranger Braddock as if he was their personal ranger. They decided the resort and town around it were far more important than Ripple Creek. Dalton was constantly being called up the mountain to take care of some trivial problem.

Ingrid picked up the microphone that had been set up with a small, scratchy sound system. She tapped the mic a few times and then lifted it to speak. "Good morning, everyone. This is quite the crowd. Thank you all for coming, and please, feel free to take photos and post them on social media." Ingrid read off the names of this year's contestants and made special mention that last year's champion, Emery Gladstone, had returned hoping for yet another victory. She took the time to thank the bakery for the pies and then she turned to the contestants. "Our pie eaters may take their seats."

"Wait," Thomas yelled from his end of the table. He scowled down at all the pies. "All of us have a great deal of whipped cream, but Emery's pie hardly has any."

Jack and I stretched to our toes. Thomas was right. While the other pies had at least four inches of white, fluffy cream, Emery's pie was nearly flat. Emery seemed to agree, but Ingrid was confused.

She held onto the microphone to address the contestants. "I don't understand how that's possible. I used the stopwatch on my phone as I sprayed each pie. Everyone got fifteen seconds of steady cream."

"Clearly something went amiss when you sprayed Emery's pie," Thomas argued. The other contestants nodded in agreement.

"I don't want to be accused of cheating," Emery looked pointedly at Thomas. "Ms. Engalls, could you please add another fifteen seconds of cream to my pie."

"Then it won't be even," Ingrid insisted.

Emery's chest puffed out, and he lifted his chin. "I don't mind having the handicap. I'm the champ, after all." The last comment caused Thomas to roll his eyes.

Ingrid walked over to an ice chest and pulled out a can of cream. She shook it vigorously as she walked the length of the table and stopped at Emery's pie. She took out her phone, swiped her thumb over it and sprayed the cream for fifteen seconds. Now Emery's pie had far more cream than the other pies.

With the whipped cream inconsistencies taken care of, it was time to start the contest. The pie eaters sat behind their pies and waited for the whistle. You could hear pine needles dropping off the trees as everyone waited in great suspense for Ingrid to blow her whistle. The sound split the air, causing a few ravens to take off from a nearby spruce.

The contestants dove right in. People started cheering for their favorites as whipped cream splattered everything within a five-foot radius. A few contestants were still working on their mound of whipped cream as Thomas and Emery reached the important part—the pie. A few contestants stopped occasionally to blow cream out of their noses.

Jack laughed. "Looks like the champ and his main competition just about have this wrapped up."

Everyone's focus was on the two gentlemen at the end of the table. There were too many heads in the way, so I hopped up on my toes again. It was hard to see from our angle, but it seemed Thomas's face was deeper into the pie tin. "They need an overhead camera and giant screen to let those of us on the ground know how close they are to finishing."

"You're right. Maybe they'll add that next year," Jack quipped. "From where I stand, I'd say Thomas might grab the trophy and hundred dollar prize this year. In fact, it seems the reigning champ is having a hard time getting to the bottom."

It was getting hard to hold my toe lift. (Good thing I didn't go into ballet.) I rested my hand on Jack's shoulder for support. He was right. Emery had slowed down.

Seconds later, Thomas jumped up from his chair. There was whipped cream in his hair and crumbs all over his face. "I won. I finished."

Ingrid's heels struck the ground with self-assured force as she strode over to judge whether or not Thomas was indeed finished. She surveyed the pie tin and then lifted it to show the crowd that he'd eaten all of it. Loud cheers filled the air.

The other contestants seemed somewhat relieved that they didn't have to continue. Diedre started untying hands. Emery finally pulled his face free from the tin. Whipped cream stuck to his eyebrows and chin. His eyes drifted shut, and his mouth pulled down in a frown. It seemed he was thoroughly disappointed that Thomas won.

Diedre moved behind Emery and waited for him to stand so she could untie his hands, but Emery stayed seated. His eyes opened for a second, then his entire body leaned to the side, and he fell out of the chair and landed on the ground with a thud. Diedre screamed.

The crowd gasped and then fell silent. We all waited for Emery to sit up and laugh or do something to show that he was joking, but he didn't move.

"That doesn't look good," Jack said.

"Everyone, out of the way." I zeroed in on the voice in the crowd. It was Dr. Schaffer. He had a practice about three miles north of Ripple Creek, and a lot of locals used him as their GP. People parted so he could make his way to the table.

In the meantime, Ingrid had taken up the microphone again. "Please, everyone, it seems as if Mr. Gladstone has fainted. Let's step back and allow Dr. Schaffer to help him."

"I've seen people faint before," Jack said. He looked at me.

"I agree. He didn't faint. In fact, it almost looks as if he's…"

Jack nodded in agreement.

"I think I'll stick around for a short while to see if my help is needed."

"I'll get back to the bakery. Call if you need anything." Jack took off, and I walked around the outside of the concerned onlookers toward the table. Thomas Anderson looked slightly stunned and kind of miffed. It seemed his big moment had been completely overshadowed by Emery's collapse. Was Emery pretending? Was he that upset about losing that he faked a health issue?

Dr. Schaffer spent a few seconds tapping lightly on Emery's cheek. "Emery, Emery, it's me, Dr. Schaffer." After a few seconds of no response, the doctor picked up Emery's limp wrist and searched for a pulse. Schaffer's shoulders rounded, and he removed the hat from his head and placed it over his chest. That caused another gasp to whip through the crowd. It seemed this was a pie contest that people would be talking about long past the holidays. Emery Gladstone, last year's champion, was dead.

eleven

...

INGRID WAS SCURRYING around in her gray suit and heels trying to decide what to do to avoid utter chaos. The pie eating contest had ended in a shocking tragedy, with the pie eating favorite falling over dead at the table. I tried not to think about the fact that my pie was the last thing he ate before he keeled over.

"I've sent a text to Ranger Braddock letting him know he's needed right away at the park," I told a very frantic Ingrid. "He's probably close by." My phone beeped. I lifted it. "The ranger is on his way." That seemed to calm her.

Dr. Schaffer stayed with the body. "I'd tell this crowd to be on their way. I'm sure Ranger Braddock will be calling the coroner, and there'll need to be an investigation."

Ingrid's hand flew to her chest. "Surely not. I mean, what would they investigate? The poor man is dead, right?"

"He's dead all right." Schaffer stuck his hat back on his mound of wispy white hair. Respectfulness took a backseat

A Pie For A Pie

when there was a chill in the air. "Just not sure why."

"His skin tone looks ruddy and blotchy," I pointed out.

Schaffer nodded. "Yes, it's odd. And his skin is warm to the touch. He hasn't been dead long, so I wouldn't expect him to be cold yet, but his skin is unusually warm, especially given this morning's temperature."

"Did he choke?" Ingrid asked. "I'm always worried about that in this silly contest. It's not safe—gobbling food at such a fast pace and all without coming up for a breath."

Dr. Schaffer adjusted the scarf around his neck. "It seems he would have given us some kind of indication that he was choking. Still, it's a possibility. But that doesn't explain the red blotches on his face."

"Maybe he was allergic to something in the pie," I suggested. "Cinnamon or eggs?"

"I was his doctor, and he never mentioned having any allergy to food. Might have been his heart."

"That's right," Ingrid said. "He told me he had a heart attack three years ago. I ran into him at the drugstore one day, and we got into a long discussion about health and supplements. He said he was taking much better care of himself since his heart attack."

I looked at the doctor. "He was in much better shape in the last few years. The heart attack wasn't a bad one, but it scared him. Still, I suppose it's possible his heart gave out. Doesn't really explain the skin blotches or warm skin."

"It seemed he slowed down on the pie eating just as he was about to finish the contest," I said. "Maybe he was in pain. He couldn't clutch his chest because his hands were tied."

Dr. Schaffer looked as shaken as Ingrid. "Dear, dear me. Certainly didn't expect this. I thought it would be fun to come down and watch the contest. Never expected it to end like this."

Ingrid made a sort of snorting sound. "You can say that again. The council is going to be gutted. And heaven knows what they're saying about the event on social media." As she said it, Diedre hurried over with her phone clutched in her hand. Ingrid's face turned white as she looked at it.

"'Deadly pumpkin pie' is trending," Ingrid announced.

My stomach sank. I was hoping the pumpkin pie wasn't going to become the focus, but too late—the whole thing was going to be blamed on the delicious pumpkin pies Jack and I baked. My bakery would take a hit, too, and I was sure the old adage that all publicity was good publicity didn't hold up when your bakery was credited with baking a deadly pie.

Ingrid walked over to talk to Diedre. She looked shaken, but she eventually walked over and took hold of a trash can. She dragged it over to the table. It seemed Ingrid had told her to start cleaning up the mess. I hurried over. "No, Ingrid, I'm sorry. You need to leave everything exactly as it is. Ranger Braddock may have to collect evidence."

Again, Ingrid's face lost color. This time she went gray like her suit. "Evidence? I don't understand. Don't they collect evidence if it's a murder? We were all standing right here. We witnessed the poor man's death. How could it possibly be a murder?"

I had no intention of telling her what had been traipsing through my brain for the past few minutes. If Emery had been poisoned, then my pie had been used as a vehicle for that poison, and I didn't want to think about that.

"Trust me, Ranger Braddock will want the entire scene untouched, no matter what the cause of death."

Ingrid turned to Diedre. "Leave everything in place. You can go home. Thank you for your help." She turned back to me. "Can I at least put my coolers and the chairs in my truck?"

I shook my head. "I'm afraid not." I glanced toward the road. "There's Ranger Braddock now. He'll let you know when you can pack up." A morning debrief with Dalton was the last thing I'd hoped for, but it had to be done. I walked toward his truck to meet him.

He had his notebook and phone out. "Scottie, I was up at the resort." (Could have guessed that.) "What's going on?"

We kept walking toward the table, and it didn't take him long to see the focus of the problem. "Is that—?"

"Emery Gladstone. The contest ended with Thomas Anderson as the winner. Emery had slowed down considerably at the end. Then he sat up, closed his eyes, and a few seconds later he fell to the side. Dr. Schaffer was here to confirm that he was dead."

Dalton looked over at me. "Dead? From the pie?"

I smiled smugly at him. "Yes, thanks for jumping right to that conclusion. I assure you my pies are perfectly harmless. Unless you eat too many." Something had shifted. I expected us to be back in our awkward dance, but as soon as I saw him, I reminded myself that it was Dalton, the boy I'd grown up with and the man I'd become close to again. The only thing missing was that constant butterfly flutter that had plagued me since my return to Ripple Creek. The butterflies had left. I was talking to a friend now, and I hoped that was how things would stay.

Dalton reached the body. Dr. Schaffer shook his hand. "Thanks for coming, Ranger Braddock. I'm not sure what we're looking at here. Knowing his medical history, I strongly considered that Mr. Gladstone died of a heart attack—what with the excitement and energy of the contest this morning. But there are some inconsistencies—his blotchy skin for one."

"Severe allergic reaction?" Dalton suggested.

Dr. Schaffer rubbed his bearded chin. "Always a possibility, only I didn't know of any allergies. The coroner will want to perform an autopsy. He'll let you know if this was a natural death or something else."

That last statement caught Dalton's attention. "Something else?"

"I realize there were numerous witnesses to his death, and from what we all saw—Mr. Gladstone ate his pie, sat up and then died." Dr. Schaffer looked at the mostly empty pie plate. "Ms. Ramone wisely instructed Ms. Engalls to leave everything in place."

The doctor's meaning became clearer, and it seemed he was coming to the same possible conclusion as me.

Dalton glanced at the table and the pie plates. "Do you think he was poisoned?"

Dr. Schaffer didn't want to commit either way. "Let's just say, it's a possibility. Now, I've got to head back to my office to do some paperwork. Please don't hesitate to call if you need me."

Dalton nodded. "Thank you for your time. I'll call if I have further questions." Dr. Schaffer went one direction, and Dalton walked the other with his phone at his ear. It was time to call the coroner. We could guess about the cause of death all morning, but we wouldn't know anything for certain until after the coroner's exam.

I circled behind the table. I stood behind Emery's chair and stared down into the pie pan. Every pie had been made the same way. I fretted knowing this was not going to look good for the bakery. As my eyes dropped, I noticed something on the outside of the pie tin. Someone had drawn an X with black marker on the side of the tin. I quickly glanced at the other pie plates on the table. Only Emery's had the black X.

I pulled out my phone and called Jack. He answered on one ring.

"What's going on? Have they figured out the cause of death?"

"Not yet. We'll need the coroner."

Jack paused. "Gee, Scottie, do you think it was the pie?"

"Not unless Emery had some dreadful food allergy he forgot to mention. The doctor didn't see any signs of choking either. Hey, Jack, you didn't by any chance mark one of the pie tins with a black X, did you?"

"A black X? No. Why would I do that?"

"Just curious. I see one on the pie plate Emery ate from."

"That's suspicious. Do you think it was murder?" Jack asked.

"I'm beginning to think that might be the case. It seems someone decided to use one of our beautiful pies as part of their sinister plan."

twelve

. . .

"IT'S PROBABLY best if you leave the scene to the officials," Dalton said. He was avoiding eye contact, so it seemed we were back to the awkward dance, only this was for a whole different reason.

"My pies are perfectly safe to eat," I said sharply.

"I know." He finally made eye contact, and frankly, having his gaze resting on my face, didn't help my resolve to stay on defense. "Let me handle this. I'm sure you've got work to do in the bakery."

"Oh, you mean the bakery where I bake deadly treats?" I gave my beanie a tug, turned hard on my heels and walked away.

"Scottie, I'm just doing my job," he called to me.

I waved curtly back at him and continued toward the bakery. Jack was refilling the flour container. White dust floated in the air around him. "Any more news?" He lowered the sack of flour.

"No, but as a little bonus to the morning, 'deadly pumpkin

pie' is trending on social media."

"Terrific," he muttered. "Maybe we should stick with apple pie this season?" He added a smile to show me he was, of course, kidding.

"With Thanksgiving next week, we've already got a dozen orders for pumpkin pies," I said.

Jack's face dropped. It was a habit of his when he didn't want to tell me something.

"Jack?"

His big round shoulders bunched up. "Three people have cancelled their pie orders this morning."

"So, the fallout has begun. Soon, word will be up and down the mountain that we bake deadly pies."

"I'm sure it will all blow over in a few weeks."

I raised a brow at him. "But in the meantime, we're going to be stuck with twenty cans of pumpkin and no pie orders to fill." The front door opened.

It was Esme from the bookshop. "What on earth is happening? I was in my stockroom putting prices on a new shipment of books when I heard a lot of people walking back from the park excitedly discussing a death. Who died?"

"Jack, is it all right if I step next door with Esme for a few minutes? I'll tell her all the excitement of the morning." I had some other news to talk about as well. Esme was my sounding board when it came to men.

Jack waved us on.

"Oh, good, I received those vintage cookbooks you ordered. They're somewhere in the boxes of new books," Esme said as we stepped out and around to her shop. The coroner's van rolled past just as we shut the door behind us. "So, someone did die?" Esme asked.

"Emery Gladstone. He was in the pie eating contest."

"Did he choke?" I followed Esme to her storeroom. Three big boxes sat open on the floor, and stacks of new books sat around waiting for their shelf space. "I think your cookbooks are in that box." She pointed and then sat behind the adjacent box. "I once sat through a pepper eating contest, and one contestant collapsed. His face was bright red, and he was in so much pain he bent over and fell on the floor. He was all right though. I thought he'd choked, but it turned out he just couldn't take the heat." She giggled. "A little pepper-eating pun." She smiled my direction, and her chin dropped. "Sorry. You're upset about it. It must have been shocking to see."

"It's not that, although, yes, it was a shock. But Emery wasn't choking. He ate my pie and then fell over dead. Not a good look for the bakery." Esme's three cats joined us as we sat on the floor amongst the books. Earl, my favorite, rubbed his chubby gray body around me a few times and then plopped down next to me.

"Nonsense. They can't possibly blame your pie unless he had a food allergy, then it would be his fault for not checking the ingredients."

"I don't know, Esme. I always find myself in the most chaotic situations."

"Uh-oh, this doesn't *all* have to do with the pie contest, does it? I assume you had to meet and talk to—you-know-who—since there was a death."

"I did and things are still a little strained between us, but the real chaos has to do with Cade."

Esme put down the books she was holding. "What happened? Wait. Is he back in town?"

"He is, only he didn't tell me. I went up to his house, and

there was a noise and light inside. I thought it was an intruder. It turned out Cade was back and then I basically confessed my love for him, although not in such poetic terms."

Esme clapped. "Yay, so it finally happened. I knew it was destined to be. You can practically see static electricity in the air around you two whenever you're together."

"Really? I guess I always knew there was a strong connection. I missed him terribly when he was in Europe."

"So, that's it, then? You two are on your way to being an official couple? By the way, his latest book has sold out everywhere. I'm expecting another shipment soon, and there's a list of people waiting for it."

"That's exciting. I know the sales really took off once he started out on tour." I reached into the box and pulled out a stack of historical romances. I set them on the floor. "Unfortunately, the couple scenario has hit a snag, and it's an aggravating one because it was all a misunderstanding. Cade showed up at the house last night just as Dalton was leaving with the tin of oatmeal cookies my grandmother had baked him. Cade got back into his car and left without a word. I sent an angry text, and he hasn't written back. I might just have had the world's shortest relationship with the man."

"Nonsense, it'll be fine." Esme reached into the box. "Oh, I was wrong. Your books are in this box. These are reprints, but I'm still looking for some actual vintage copies like you asked."

"I love to see what people wrote in the margins, little notes about what to add or tips for making the treats better." Esme handed me the books *Cookies Galore* and *The Latest Cake Secrets*. Both books were from the mid-twentieth century when electric mixers were the new rage and women spent their day in aprons and high heels. Or at least that was what I envisioned. I loved the old-fashioned art and photos that went with recipes for things like cocoa rolls, fig envelopes, banana fritters and even peanut brittle. "Some methods and ingredient combos back then were questionable, but most of our modern recipes had roots in all of these cookbooks. Thanks so much for ordering them. I can't wait to browse through them."

"You're welcome, and I'll keep an eye out for originals." Esme stacked a few more books on the floor. "What will you do now?"

"You mean about Cade?"

She nodded.

"I'll wait to hear from him. I sent the angry text and I regret it, but at the same time, I think I had every right to be mad. He left without giving me a chance to explain. He came upon a perfectly innocent situation but immediately read it the way he wanted. Dalton lives in this town. He adores my grandmother, and he loves my bakery treats. At least he did before this morning's disaster. I can't avoid him entirely, so Cade will either have to accept it, or we're through before we even began."

"No, don't say that. It was meant to be. I'm sure of it. Give him some time." Esme sighed as she looked around at the stack of books. "What an exciting life I lead. This is my Sunday morning."

"Do you need some help?"

"No, I've got a method to all this madness, only it's too wacky to explain to anyone else."

I rubbed Earl's ears for a moment. "I think I'll walk to the park to see if there's any word about Emery's death." I stopped before leaving the stockroom. "By the way, does Diedre still come in here to study?"

"DeeDee? Yes, she comes in a lot. Why do you ask?"

"She was at the disastrous pie contest. I plan to talk to Ingrid, and since Diedre was helping this morning, I should talk to her, too."

"That's right. She mentioned she'd be working at the contest. I'm not exactly sure where she lives, but I could ask her."

"Or just let me know if she happens to come into the bookstore. It'll seem less contrived if I just happen to meet her in the shop."

"You've got it. See you later."

I waved the book. "I'm going to leave these at the counter and pick them up on my way back from the park."

"Good luck."

"Yep, I'll need it. Dalton dismissed me rather coldly earlier, but if this was murder, then I've got a big stake in it. Or, I should say, a big pumpkin pie."

thirteen

. . .

THE CORONER and his team were about to place Emery in a body bag. Dalton was wearing gloves and carefully sliding pie tins, complete with half-eaten pies, into evidence bags. I hurried over to let him know about the X on Emery's pie plate. He glanced up from his task with a serious expression. He didn't look pleased to see me.

"I know," I started before he could get all bossy and official on me, "I know you told me to leave this investigation alone, but I forgot to mention something important." I glanced at the pile of filled evidence bags on the end of the table. "Did you notice anything different on Emery's pie tin?"

Dalton looked up at me. "Something different? You mean like it was tainted with poison?"

That statement wiped the cockiness out of my expression. I was ready to let him know that he missed something important, but he had bigger, more shocking news. "So, it's confirmed? Emery was poisoned?"

"Not confirmed but strongly indicated. The flushed, ruddy skin and warm body temperature indicate probable poisoning. Obviously, there will have to be an autopsy to confirm cause of death and find the type of poison." I didn't like the grim set of his jaw. It was tight, which meant he was concerned.

"Dalton, I had no reason to kill Emery Gladstone. I barely knew the man and only talked to him when he came into the bakery." I'd always helped in these murder investigations, but I'd never been on the side of possible suspect. I didn't like it much.

"Did you make the pies, or did your employee—"

"Ah, I see where this is going. You've never liked Jack."

"I never said I didn't like him."

Dalton took a deep breath. "I just strongly cautioned you about hiring a man who's done time for assault. And now that it's out in the open—did you make the pies alone or with Jack's assistance?"

I straightened my posture. However, it wasn't easy with the way I was feeling. "I see, so is this an interrogation? Do I need a lawyer?"

Dalton softened his stance, which helped me do the same. "Come on, Scottie. You of all people know how this works. I've got to talk to people with motive—"

I snapped my fingers. "See, right there. You just said it yourself. You need to talk to people with motive, and I don't fall into that category. Neither does Jack. He knew Emery even less than me."

"How do you know that for sure? I'm sure there's plenty of things you don't know about Jack."

I stood rigid again. I was back on defense. "I know he takes a splash of milk in his coffee. I know his favorite Christmas movie is 'It's a Wonderful Life' and he watches it every December with a plate of gingerbread cookies and warm milk by his side. I know he loves snowy nights but hates snowy mornings. He puts out grape jelly for the orioles in the summer, and he doesn't like to fly. His favorite book is—"

"All right. I get your point. So, you know a lot about him, and he's—"

"He's the best assistant I've ever worked with," I added.

Dalton sealed up the last pie plate. There was whipped cream smeared on the inside of the bag. "The lab is going to throw a fit. These will be a mess to deal with." He put the last bag on the pile and started bagging up the plastic aprons. Emery's apron had been removed from his body and placed in a separate bag.

"You never answered my question. Did you bake the pies alone, or did your *assistant* help?" He'd switched back to his official tone, and I couldn't help but feel his attitude toward me had more to do with our Saturday morning chat than with the possibility that Jack or I had laced a pumpkin pie with poison.

"Jack made the pie crusts. He has a special talent for making an incredibly flaky crust. I mixed the pumpkin filling, and Jack filled and baked the pies. It was a joint effort, and you may come any time to search my kitchen for poison. I take food safety and cleanliness very seriously in my bakery."

The coroner team lifted the body bag onto a gurney. "Looks like they're ready to leave."

"Have I answered all of your questions sufficiently, Ranger Braddock?" He winced at the tone I used, but I couldn't help myself. I supposed this was how everyone felt being interrogated about a murder, only most people didn't know the interrogator as well as I knew Dalton.

A Pie For A Pie

"Yes, fine. Really, Scottie, I'm just doing my job. Someone fed Emery Gladstone a pie with poison, and it resulted in his death."

"What if Emery had been poisoned earlier, before the contest, and it only took hold after he finished the pie?"

"Good point and I plan to talk to people who spoke with Emery before the contest. Maybe they noticed something was off —like slurred speech or a flushed complexion."

I immediately thought back to my walk around the lake. I'd spoken to Emery. He seemed fine. He was happy and energized and ready to eat pie—my poisonous pie, apparently. Dalton noticed a change in my countenance.

"Scottie? Did you have something to add?" I decided not to mention that Emery seemed fine before the contest. After all, what did I know? I hardly knew the man. "Just a few things— June Greene is Emery's longtime girlfriend."

Dalton pulled out his notepad and read the name June Greene. "Yes, as far as Ingrid Engalls knew, June was his next of kin. I'm going to talk to her once I'm done here."

"Well, there was trouble in paradise. June wanted Emery to propose, and she gave him an ultimatum—marriage or they were through. He didn't want to discuss it because he was too focused on the contest."

Dalton's mouth tilted in a grin. "Lots of information for someone who didn't know the victim well," he noted.

"Well, they discussed it in the bakery and then I heard June telling Roxi about the ultimatum when she—"

Dalton put up his hand. "Stop. I'm kidding. I know how people in this town talk. A proposal ultimatum would be like prime beef in the world of gossip." Dalton stepped a little closer. He smelled like cloves and cinnamon from the pie tins. "Look, Scottie, I know you had nothing to do with this, but I have to come at this from a professional angle…not a friendship angle."

"I know. And Dalton, Jack's such a good guy. Really."

He nodded.

"How did things go after I left last night?" Dalton asked. "Rafferty looked upset."

This was not a topic change I wanted. I already missed the interrogation. "I'm not sure. He obviously didn't love seeing you at my door. That's all right. I'll get it straightened."

The door on the coroner's van slammed shut, pulling our attention that direction.

"I've got to talk to them before they take off." He started that way, then stopped and spun around with a teasing smile. "In the meantime, Ms. Ramone—don't leave town."

I shook my head. I was supposed to stay out of this one, but I felt more pulled into it than ever. I needed to clear the reputation of my pumpkin pie. As I headed back to the bakery, I tried to pull up the entire scene at the park this morning. There were so many people, both local and from out of town, at the contest, but I tried to narrow it down to the few people I knew had some connection to Emery Gladstone. I'd noticed right away that June Greene wasn't in the crowd. I'd written it off as an angry girlfriend waiting for some kind of response on her ultimatum. Or maybe she'd gotten one. Maybe Emery had told her he was going to take the offramp rather than the wedding aisle. Maybe June was angry enough to poison Emery. There'd been plenty of time between the contest setup and the actual pie eating for someone to slip poison into the pie. I grunted in frustration. Dalton had me so aggravated, I'd forgotten to tell him about the black X. It had to mean something.

My mind rolled back to this morning. Hannah had told us that Emery was having a feud with his neighbor, Marge Bivens, about her hens and his dog. Marge had been at the park when I arrived, but I couldn't remember seeing her once the contest started. Of course, I hadn't really been searching her out, and there was a large group. It would have been hard to keep track of her even if I was trying.

Thomas Anderson had also been in somewhat of a feud with Emery. It seemed they'd taken competition to a new, ugly level over the contest. And then there were Emery's last words to me—possibly his last words period. He told me he thought Thomas was planning to cheat to win the trophy. He didn't know how, and I couldn't see a way to cheat in front of a large crowd. Poisoning one's opponent seemed especially drastic. Had Thomas put something in the pie hoping it would slow Emery down, only it resulted in his death?

Lots of questions to answer and people to see. The reputation of my bakery was on the line.

fourteen

. . .

JACK HAD GOTTEN everything prepared for reopening the bakery Tuesday. He truly was a treasure. I sent him home early and decided to get some paperwork finished in the office. Unfortunately, financial spreadsheets weren't enough to hold my attention. It didn't help that my stomach was growling. The crazy morning had made me hungry. I let Nana know I wouldn't be home for lunch. Instead, I headed across the street to the market. I knew Roxi came in for a few hours on Sunday to cut ingredients for Monday's sandwiches. Hopefully, I'd find her still busy behind the deli counter.

I looked toward the park. I could see most of the parking lot from the center of the road. Dalton's truck was gone. No doubt he was telling June Greene the bad news. June was my main reason for my market visit. That, and, the possibility of a ham and cheese sandwich in the refrigerator.

There were no customers when I walked in. Roxi's knife tapped the cutting board, and the smell of red onions filled the air. "I'll be right with you," she called, not knowing it was me. In the summer, Roxi had four to five employees working in the market, but once winter reared its blustery head, the summer help either returned to school or went back down the hill. She always had a hard time finding anyone to work during the bad weather months, and that proved a problem during the holidays. Poor Roxi ended up spending most of her time manning the store all by herself.

She glanced up from her task as I neared the deli counter. "Scottie, it's you." She put down the knife and slid the pungent onion slices into their container. "I heard it was quite the pie contest. Poor Ingrid came in here to buy a bottle of wine. She said she was going to spend the rest of the day drinking wine, watching old movies and wiping this morning from her mind. I assume you can tell me more concise details. Ingrid was rambling on about pies and whipped cream and the ridiculous demands of her job on city council."

"I'm afraid there's not much to tell at this point. Emery was eating his pie. Thomas won and then Emery fell over dead."

Roxi waited eagerly for more and then realized I was finished. "So much for those concise details I was counting on." She pulled a large tomato out of a bowl and started to slice it. She paused to look up at me. "If Emery was eating your pie—"

"Yes, it's true, my poor pumpkin pie has just had its reputation marred by Emery's unfortunate demise. Along that line, Roxi, how well do you know June Greene?"

"June? Poor thing. She'll be torn up about this. I've known June for about ten years. We used to go to the same hairstylist and, of course, she comes into the market several times a week. She always tells me about everything going on in her life. I might be checking out groceries, but sometimes I feel like a bartender behind that cash register."

"Do you know what happened with June's ultimatum? She was talking about it in here yesterday morning?"

Roxi squinted an eye at me. "Is this part of an investigation?" Her eyes widened. "Was it murder? I just assumed the man choked or died of a heart attack. See, and this is why I need details."

"There hasn't been any confirmed cause of death yet. I'm sure the coroner will have that soon. Dalton will need to know if this is a murder investigation or if Emery died of natural causes. That said—there were some indications that he was poisoned. Of course, don't share that with anyone at your *bar* counter." I added a wink.

"Poison," Roxi repeated. "Never would have guessed that. But again, wasn't he eating your pie?"

"Yes, unfortunately. And thank you for driving that point home. But I assure you my pumpkin pies left the bakery as perfectly harmless pies."

"Of course."

"Still, it's not a good look for my bakery business. Come to Scottie's for the pie. Leave in a box—and not a pink one." I gave my head a shake. "Don't know why I said that. I guess my mind is a little scrambled. Back to June—did you hear any more about the ultimatum? June mentioned that Emery refused to talk about it until after the contest."

Roxi started cutting more tomatoes. "That's right. June was really upset that their relationship had taken the back seat to a pie eating contest. I hadn't spoken to her since she was in here telling us about her ultimatum, but Regina came in later yesterday afternoon. She'd spoken to Becky, who knows June well, and she told Regina that June was planning to leave

Emery. June was really broken up about his lack of commitment, and she worried she was wasting too many good years with the man."

"I'm on her side there. I wasted many years with Jonathan and then when it was time to get married, I realized it had been the wrong thing for me all along." I waved a hand. "Obviously, I needed to get that small morsel off my chest. I'm sure it has to do with—" I shook my head. "Never mind."

"I hear things aren't going well between Dalton and Crystal." Roxi set down the knife and slid the tomatoes into their container. "In fact, my source for that rumor is solid. Dalton told me himself," Roxi said.

I looked at her in surprise.

Roxi pretended to whip a towel off her shoulder and wipe the inside of an invisible glass. "What'll it be," she asked with a growl. "A house beer or one of those imported wines?" She laughed. "I kid you not. I stand back here innocently ringing up orders of pretzels and orange juice and people tell me all their personal problems. Dalton usually only confides in me when no one else is in the store, but I can tell you, from knowing him for such a long time, that he's not a happy person."

"I know and I feel bad for him, but he'll figure it out." I didn't want to get any further into the subject. Besides, I was sure Nana would fill Roxi in during their next chat at the coffee shop. "Do you think June would be upset enough, and, I suppose I should add in, crazy enough to poison Emery?" I wasn't usually so bold about tossing out my murder theories, but I wanted to get this one solved and hopefully before Thanksgiving.

Roxi wiped her hands on her apron. "Gosh, I don't think so. I mean June can be dramatic, but I think deep down she still cared for Emery. They'd been together a long time, and even if you cut someone out of your life, you still have feelings for them. Of course, what do I know? I'm just a bartender." She laughed. "Maybe I should open up a bar counter on the other side of the store."

"Oh, speaking of the other side of the store—do you still have some sandwiches left? I need some lunch."

"I think there might be a few left. Business has been slow."

I headed to the back of the store to the freshly made sandwiches. I was in luck. There was a ham and cheese on pumpernickel left. My favorite. I carried it up to the register.

"What about Thomas Anderson?" Roxi asked.

"What about him?"

"He was in here last week telling everyone he was going to win the contest and that Emery's championship reign was over. Maybe he was trying to make sure he won. Especially after all that boasting."

"That's crossed my mind. It seems like a big leap for a motive, but people do crazy things."

I paid for the sandwich. "Are you still working across the street, or are you going to take some much-needed time off?" Roxi asked.

I glanced around at her store. She was the only person working. "Seems like you should be asking yourself that question."

"You're right. Sure wish I could find someone like Jack to help out in the store."

"I can't thank my lucky stars enough for having that man walk into my bakery."

fifteen

. . .

THE HAM and cheese sandwich hit the spot, and I was able to push the morning from my mind long enough to get paperwork done. Cade had not texted or called all day. I'd had to talk myself out of calling him. He was the one who drove away without so much as a word. I'd made the last move—my angry and regrettable text—so it was his move. If he was going to be this sensitive about things, then I wasn't sure we could be a couple. As Esme pointed out, his newest book was doing very well. Maybe he no longer wanted to live in our small town. Maybe after spending time in Paris and London, he decided he was far more worldly than Ripple Creek. I couldn't blame him. This town didn't offer much more than beautiful scenery, fresh air and a close-knit community. It was enough for some of us but not for everyone. Those conclusions left me feeling glum. I didn't want Cade to leave. I wanted him here, in Ripple Creek, with me.

My phone beeped with a text, and I scrambled to grab it,

hoping that through some sort of Star Trek-style mind meld I'd prompted Cade to text me. It was Dalton.

"I saw the light on in the kitchen. I'm at the door."

It took me a second to get over the disappointment that the text wasn't from Cade. I walked to the door. Dalton took off his hat and stepped inside. "I thought I'd drop by and let you know—I've heard from the coroner. Initial lab results show that Emery's blood contained the alkaloids atropine and scopolamine from Atropa belladonna. It's a deadly nightshade plant. There was enough in his blood to cause his already weakened heart to kick into overdrive. He essentially died of a heart attack that was brought on by the poison."

"Wow, that's awful."

Dalton's gaze dropped.

"There's more," I said.

His head dipped slightly in a half-hearted nod. "There was still enough pie on Emery's plate for the lab. It tested positive for the same alkaloids."

"Well, then someone added it to Emery's pie before the contest. Wait, we never finished our earlier conversation. Someone had drawn an X in black marker on the foil pie pan. It was only on Emery's pie plate. And it didn't leave the bakery that way."

"I saw the X. Ingrid said only Jack was in the bakery this morning when she picked up the pies."

I blew out an exasperated puff of air. "Jack had no reason to kill Emery Gladstone. Someone wrote that X on the pie after it left the bakery. I even checked with Jack this morning after I noticed it. He didn't write it. Those pies were set on that table when I reached the park this morning. Someone tampered with that pie before the contest, and they marked it to make sure that

A Pie For A Pie

particular pie ended up in Emery's spot. The champion always gets the first position on the table. Everyone knows that."

Dalton didn't reply.

"Oh my gosh, just out with it," I snapped.

"The lab said all parts of the plant are poisonous. Someone had to blend up the plant with water to make it liquid. But how did it get into the pie?"

I shrugged sharply. My impatience was growing. He was determined to pin this on Jack, and I wasn't going to let that happen. "I have no idea. If it was in liquid form, maybe it was injected into the pie."

Dalton didn't look convinced by my theory. "I read up on the plant. The berries have a slightly sweet taste. They appear at this time of year, but I can't help wondering why Emery didn't taste that something was off with the pie."

"That's easy. It was a pie eating contest. Everyone was eating at a frenzied pace. I could have put a load of salt in those pies, and no one would have paused to ask why the pie was salty. It was all about digging their faces in and getting to that last piece of crust. Even if Emery had thought the pie tasted funny, he never would have stopped to mention it. He wanted to win… badly. So did Thomas Anderson. Have you spoken to Thomas? He had motive."

"I don't know if wanting to win a pie eating contest can be considered motive," Dalton said with a half-smile.

"Normally, I'd agree, only those two men have been acting as if they were about to compete in the Olympics. And Thomas was at the park early. He had motive and proximity."

"I'm going to talk to him and Ingrid Engalls, too. I need to know the exact timeline of her morning. Look, Scottie, I'm going to be talking to Jack, too."

"Fine. Do what you need to do. In the meantime, I'll find out who put poison in that pie."

Dalton's expression grew serious. "Leave this one to me. If this does have something to do with Jack—"

"It doesn't," I said sharply.

Dalton sighed. "I came here as a courtesy, to let you know that the pie contained poison and that the poison caused Emery's death."

I headed toward the door to let him know we were through talking. "Yes, well, thank you for that courtesy."

Dalton walked out but stopped and looked back at me. This time there was no sternness, no warning about staying clear in his face. He looked sad, almost broken. It had nothing to do with the case. Dalton had been confiding in Roxi that he was unhappy in his relationship with Crystal and then I'd let him know that we were never going to be anything more than friends. Even that felt tenuous, especially with this case landing solidly between us. His expression broke my heart, but I didn't know what to say to him to make him feel better. He'd have to figure this one out on his own. I hoped for his sake he'd figure it out sooner rather than later. He turned and walked away. There was a definite slump in his posture.

I locked the door and went back to the office. I glanced at my phone. Darn Cade for abandoning me when I needed him. Not that he had any idea what was going on in town. It was another sign that he probably wanted nothing more to do with Ripple Creek. He rarely ventured into town. People knew who he was, but aside from me and a casual acquaintance with Esme and Roxi, he hadn't struck up any other friendships. Maybe he realized he wouldn't be here long enough to bother.

I pushed those thoughts from my mind. I had something

more important to worry about. I picked up the phone and called Jack. I hated to bother him on his afternoon off, but he needed to know what was happening.

"Hey, Scottie, anything wrong?" Jack was always ready to lend a helping hand whenever I needed it. Along with being one heck of a coworker, he was a true friend.

"I'm sorry to bother you, Jack."

His chortle rumbled through the phone. "What could I possibly be doing of importance? Although I did watch a thirty-minute video on growing your own vanilla pods. It's not going to work up here in the Rockies, but maybe, someday, when I relocate to Madagascar. So, what's up?"

"The coroner found poison from the belladonna plant in Emery's bloodstream and in our pie."

"Belladonna, wow. Didn't expect that. Was that all it took to kill him?"

"Apparently there was enough to kill him because he already had a bad heart. Then, with the excitement of the contest—I don't know. I'm not a doctor, but we witnessed it ourselves. Emery died after eating the pie."

"Oh boy, that's not good. Dalton doesn't actually think we poisoned it, does he?" His chuckle ended abruptly. "No, he would never think you did it, but your ex-con assistant—now that's someone to look at. Right?"

"I'm sorry, Jack. I told him he was wasting his time. I just wanted to give you the heads up in case he dropped by to talk to you."

"Right. Thanks for the warning. Of course, I was in the shop all morning alone, so my alibi isn't great. How did someone get poison into the pie?"

"Coroner thought the plant parts were blended into a liquid."

"That would make more sense, and it would be less noticeable." Jack sighed. The dejection pulsed through the phone. "That's the problem when you've found yourself on the wrong side of the law. Everyone always thinks you're just one hop away from landing back there. Only I never want to see the inside of a cell again. Don't worry, Scottie. This will get cleared up soon enough."

"Yes," I said with renewed determination. "It will. And I'm going to see that it does."

sixteen

. . .

I WOKE to the phone ringing. It was Monday, the one day I could truly sleep in. And after tossing and turning all night, I'd finally coasted into restful sleep. The incessant sound became part of my dream where I was desperately looking for my ringing phone. I opened my eyes and realized the ringing was real. So was the buttery smell of pancakes cooking on the griddle. Nana noticed my sour mood the night before and promised to make pancakes in the morning.

I grabbed the phone, hoping it wasn't Dalton with more bad news. Surprisingly, it was Cade. I sat up and smoothed my hair as if he could somehow see me through the phone. "Hello."

There was a long pause. "I'm a toad," he said dryly.

"No argument there."

"I'm not worthy," he continued.

"Again, no argument."

"I'm sorry. Everything was so fresh still, so new. I saw Dalton at your house and immediately—"

"You immediately thought the worst, but if you'd been brave enough to come up to the house, I would have explained that Dalton dropped by for cookies. My grandmother had spotted him in town looking sad, so she made him his favorite oatmeal cookies. I didn't even know he was coming."

"I don't know what to say—except, I repeat—I'm a toad."

"Yes, but I'm hoping eventually I can kiss you into princedom."

"I certainly look forward to that. Wait. Aren't *frogs* the ones who eventually become princes?"

"They're all amphibians."

"Are you free today? I thought maybe I could make up for my boorish behavior with some lunch. Although I have to go to the store first. My cupboards are bare."

"I'm not sure I can make it."

"Oh," he said with heavy disappointment.

"I'm not still mad…not *too* mad anyway, but there's been a murder."

"And I should be shocked by those words, but I'm not. Who died?"

"His name is Emery Gladstone. He was in the pie eating contest."

Nana poked her head into the room. "Thought maybe you were talking to yourself." She lifted her brows in question and mouthed "Cade?" I nodded. She backed out of the room and shut the door.

"A man was murdered in the middle of a pie eating contest?" Cade asked. "Actually, it makes sense given the event took place in Ripple Creek. So, does this mean you're off to spend the day with the ranger?"

"I see we're staying with toad status for a while."

"Sorry but one thing does lend itself neatly to the next. But you're right. None of my business." A chill came through the phone.

"First of all, I'm venturing out on my own for this case. My pie has been implicated in a poisoning, so I need to clear the name of my bakery…and Jack. Secondly, Dalton lives in this town. He's friends with my grandmother and with me…sort of. The town is small, so there is no way to avoid running into each other. In addition—"

"Yep, you've made your point, Ramone. I need to get used to that. It won't be easy, but I'm going to give it my best shot."

"That didn't sound as confidence-filled as I would've hoped." The aroma of pancakes grew stronger. "I'm going to let you think about this conversation while I gobble up a stack of Nana's pancakes. I'm all in for the Cade and Scottie thing, but you're going to have to fix up the loose strings, so we don't unravel. Those are all on you."

"Understood. Now I'm going back to my toadstool to reflect. Be careful out there, Ramone. There are an inordinate number of psychos in this town."

I laughed. "Talk to you later."

"Bye."

I climbed out of bed, pushed my feet into my fuzzy slippers and plodded out to the kitchen in my pajamas. Nana had sliced strawberries for the pancakes. "That's it. I'm officially twelve again. And frankly, I'm okay with that."

"How was the phone call with Cade?" Nana placed the bottle of maple syrup on the table and sat down across from me.

"I think we've patched things up. We haven't been together long enough to have already hit a rough spot, but hopefully, we can get past the Dalton problem. I feel like I have. Now I just

London Lovett

need Cade to do the same."

"Good things never come easy. You're both mature adults." As she said it, I poured vast amounts of maple syrup over my stack of pancakes. Nana laughed. "I take that back. You are twelve again, at least at heart." She winked.

"I needed this. I've got a case to investigate."

Nana rested back. "Surely not. Is it the Emery Gladstone death? There was rumor it was a heart attack."

I chewed and shook my head. I washed the bite down with a sip of coffee. "The coroner thinks it was poison from a belladonna plant."

"Belladonna. Those are deadly. I doubt many people have those growing in their yards. They have those slightly sweet berries that attract small children. Not to mention, they're hazardous to pets."

I sat up straight. "You're right. It should be easy enough to find the killer. Whoever has a belladonna plant in their yard—"

"Only certain varieties grow in this climate," Nana said. "You'll need to know which kind of belladonna was used."

"So, there's more than one kind. Wait, I think Dalton used the word Atropa when he mentioned the poisons."

Nana rubbed her chin. "Hmm, I don't think that grows up here. You'll have to do some research."

A sharp knock on the door was followed by the front door creaking open. "Yoo-hoo?" Hannah called.

"Follow your nose to the pancakes," Nana called back.

Hannah was wearing a bright pink sweater. It matched the pink in her cheeks. "It's getting colder out there. I just finished stacking all my firewood near the back door. I'm ready for a nice, cozy winter."

Nana got Hannah a plate, and she sat for some pancakes. "I

A Pie For A Pie

wasn't expecting such a nice treat," she said.

"Sure, you were," Nana said wryly.

Hannah shrugged. "Well, maybe."

"Hannah, now that you're here—" I started, but Hannah cut me off.

"Did you hear about the death at the pie eating contest? Marge told me her neighbor just keeled over dead. She said he probably choked or something. Terrible news." She poured syrup on her pancakes.

"Actually, that's what I wanted to talk to you about," I said. "Just how bad was the feud between Marge and Emery?"

Hannah had a cheek full of pancakes. She chewed and swallowed quickly, always anxious to share gossip. "It was bad enough that they were no longer talking. Marge wrote a long letter to Emery letting him know that if one of her hens died because of his dog, then she'd be forced to hire a lawyer. It was a mostly hollow threat, of course. I told her a lawyer wouldn't be able to help her with something like that. Besides, Marge doesn't have that kind of money." Hannah took another bite and pointed to her mouth. "Yum," she muttered.

"I suppose her problems are over now," I said.

Hannah nodded. "Marge said that Emery's girlfriend, June, came and picked up the dog this morning. Marge said June was in an awful state of shock about the whole thing. Can't blame her. Who'd have thought a person could die in a pie eating contest?" Hannah wiped her mouth with a napkin and looked at me. "Wasn't that one of your pies, Scottie?"

"Yes, it was one of my pies."

"Oh, well, I'm sure his death had nothing to do with the pie," Hannah said.

"Of course, it had nothing to do with Scottie's pie," Nana said sharply. She and Hannah were good friends, but sometimes my grandmother had little patience for her neighbor.

"June told me that Emery had a bad heart," Hannah continued, completely oblivious to Nana's harsh tone. "She says his heart probably gave out. June said she begged him to eat healthier and exercise more, but he was stubborn."

"Emery didn't have much family. Who'll get the property?" I asked. I hadn't considered the possibility that someone killed Emery for an inheritance. He had a thriving business and a nice piece of property.

"I asked Marge. June said Emery left her the farm, and his half of the excavating company goes to his partner, Doug Hermann."

"Interesting." It seemed I had a few stops to make in my investigation. But first I was going to talk to Ingrid Engalls. I needed to hear her entire timeline of the morning. At some point during her hectic morning, she must have left the pies unattended, and that was when the killer made his or her move.

seventeen

. . .

INGRID ENGALLS AND HER HUSBAND, Ross, had a sweet little cabin that overlooked the creek. The creek bed was mostly dry after summer with last winter's snowmelt long gone. Pumpkins of various shapes and colors greeted me on the front porch. The porch wrapped clear around the house to the side that overlooked the creek. A massive pine shaded the right side of the house. A large silk wreath with silk maple leaves hung on the front door, and a tall wooden scarecrow leaned against the log siding with the word "welcome" written on his pitchfork. I rang the bell and a pretty tune followed.

Ingrid opened the door with enthusiasm. "I've baked some —" Some of that enthusiasm vanished along with her smile. "Scottie, hello. I was expecting my friends. We've got plans to do some quilting."

A brown sugar aroma wafted toward me. "I won't be long. Just needed to ask you a few questions."

She bit her lip. "Ranger Braddock told me you'd probably

drop by. I already told him about the morning before the pie contest. I'm sure this will all turn out to be a heart attack. What else could it be? We were all watching the contest. I wouldn't worry about it." She started to close the door.

I put my hand up to stop her and took an exaggerated whiff of the air. "Let me guess. Sticky buns—pecan, possibly?"

Ingrid's smile returned. "Wow, that's amazing. I guess with all the time you spend baking, you're an expert. They're my grandmother's recipe. She called them Molly's Extra Gooey Buns."

"I love hearing about vintage recipes that have been handed down through the generations, the tried-and-true delights from our past holidays and family get-togethers."

"I have an entire shoebox filled with her recipes. I bake her cherry-almond slab pie every Christmas. It's Ross's favorite. He waits around all day, like a kid, for it to come out of the oven." She backed up. "Come on in. I'll let you try a bun." I was stuffed from pancakes and, if I was honest, slightly sugar-drunk on maple syrup, but I'd talked my way into her home with my vintage recipe tangent. (It was a topic I would normally be thrilled to talk about if one of my own recipes wasn't about to be blacklisted by the whole town.)

"I can't wait to try one," I said. The interior of Ingrid's house was much like the exterior—homey and adorned with cute things. A large paper turkey, complete with feather tail, sat on a sideboard between two large vases of silk flowers. Her quilting squares and sewing basket were on the table.

Ingrid pointed out a stool at her kitchen island. The whole kitchen was a collage of glossy granite and maple cabinetry. Glass jars were filled with freshly cut herbs and a basket was filled with lemons and limes. Her kitchen window had a great view of the mountains. Ingrid was wearing a wide smile as she proudly carried a plate with a sticky bun to the island. I picked up the fork and carved off a piece. It was fluffy and a string of brown sugar caramel hung off the fork as I tasted it. Normally, I'd be thrilled to be eating a sticky bun, but I'd overindulged at breakfast. Still, the bun was delicious.

"So good. Really wonderful."

Ingrid was pleased. Now that I'd gotten in her good graces, I hoped I could switch topics without it being too jarring. I decided to go in from the fellow baker angle. "Ingrid, about the pie contest."

Her lips rolled in.

"Just hear me out," I said. "I know Ranger Braddock already talked to you, but this is about my pie. My reputation as the town baker is on the line. I need to find out what happened to Emery. Someone tampered with that pie."

Ingrid gave her body a little shake, and her lips unrolled. "I know people are blaming the pie, and I'm sure that's ridiculous. You're a good baker. The best this town has ever had."

I pointed at her sticky bun with my fork. "Or maybe the second best."

The flattery worked. She laughed and blushed. "So nice to hear, especially coming from you. All I can tell you is what I told Ranger Braddock yesterday afternoon." She blushed again. "Admittedly, I'd had a few glasses of wine. The whole morning had my nerves in such a state. But I think I got all the details right. Would you like some coffee with that bun?"

"No, thank you. I know you're expecting guests, so I won't stay long." I took another bite. My sugar threshold was at the very top, and I didn't even realize I had a sugar threshold until I bit into that sticky bun. "When I got to the bakery, you'd already picked up the pies."

"That's right. And Jack was so sweet. He had them all packed and ready to go. He carried them out to the truck. Then I drove down to the park. No one was there yet except a few people walking around the lake. Even the chess tables were empty. I parked the truck. Diedre hadn't arrived, but the tables had been setup. I unboxed the pies and placed them on the open tailgate of the truck. I took the cardboard nametags out of the truck and walked over to the tables to set them up. Of course, Emery was to sit at the head of the table. Then I returned to the truck. Diedre showed up, and she helped me carry the pies. We placed one behind each nametag. Then we returned to the truck to pull the chairs out. We were at the truck for a good ten minutes unloading things."

"Did you notice anyone by your truck earlier or at the table while you unloaded chairs?" I asked.

"Not that I noticed. By then, people were starting to trickle into the park for the event."

"So, the pies were unattended twice. Once when you were setting up nametags and again when you and Diedre were unloading chairs?"

"I suppose so. Actually, there was a third time they were unattended. I sent Diedre to the parking area to help people find parking spots. I'd gone back to pull out the cans of whipped cream. Ross called while I was in the truck. We spoke for a few minutes, then I returned to the table with the cans of cream. I used my phone's stopwatch and sprayed each pie with equal amounts of cream."

Her mention of whipped cream jogged my memory. "That's right. There was a problem before you blew the whistle. Thomas complained that Emery didn't have as much cream as everyone else."

"Yes, and I have no idea how that happened. I was very careful to spray each pie with an equal amount of cream."

"I believe you." It seemed something in the pie caused the cream to disintegrate. "So, the pies were unattended three different times throughout the morning."

"That's right. I certainly didn't expect anyone to tamper with them, but I suppose that's a possibility. Ranger Braddock was vague about the death when we spoke. Do you think someone put something harmful in Emery's pie? Poison?" She braced her hand on the counter. "How awful."

"I don't know for certain, but I'm trying to figure out what happened. Did you know Emery well?" I asked.

"Not really. He attended the occasional city council meeting whenever he was waiting for permits to dig on a site. I know he and Thomas had been sparring with words all week before the contest, but I assumed that was all in good fun."

"They were pretty serious about this competition." The doorbell rang. "Your friends are here. I'll get out of the way. Your sticky bun was delicious. Thank you so much."

Ingrid walked me to the door. "I think this might have been the town's last pie eating contest," she said. "It's a shame, but I don't know how we come back from something like this. The whole town watched a man die right in front of them."

"I agree, I think our pie contest days are over. Thanks again for talking to me."

I nodded politely at her friends and headed to my car. I heard a few whispers behind me about the pumpkin pie that killed Emery. This stain on my bakery wasn't going to be wiped away easily.

eighteen
...

ADMITTEDLY, I was winging it when it came to this investigation. I supposed my main goal was to stay one step ahead of the ranger. If he was wasting time with Jack, then I had the perfect opportunity to focus on some of the people who had actual motive to plan an elaborate murder. Marge Bivens was Emery's neighbor, and they'd been in a terrible feud over his dog frightening her chickens. From what Hannah told us at the kitchen table, Marge complained and even wrote a formal note threatening to hire a lawyer. Hannah also mentioned that Emery hadn't even tried to make things right. It seemed there was an easy solution to the problem. Put up a taller fence, one that the dog couldn't jump. Marge was at her wit's end about all of it. But had she been pushed far enough to kill her neighbor? I couldn't imagine Marge Bivens striking someone on the head or stabbing a person in the back, but poisoning a pie was an easy, hands-off way to commit murder.

Marge and Emery both lived on Meadowlark Lane. It was a

few miles south of town in a large swath of land that was mostly flat and, for that reason, made nice farmland. The properties in the area were surrounded by majestic mountain peaks and meadows that teemed with flowers and wildlife. It was an ideal location, and every property, even the ones with old, ramshackle farmhouses, could fetch a premium price on the real estate market. June had inherited a parcel that was worth a lot of money.

I wasn't exactly sure where Marge lived, but when I spotted a dozen fat and sassy hens clucking and scratching around the yard (no longer living in fear of the dog next door) I pulled into the driveway. Marge's house was covered in lemon yellow siding, and each window had a pair of lacey curtains drawn back and tied off with blue bows. There were a few deciduous shrubs in the front yard, all too bare from their autumn shedding to be recognized. I'd looked at a few articles about belladonna. There were several subspecies, but the most dangerous one, the one Dalton had mentioned, preferred a warm, humid climate, the opposite of Ripple Creek's climate. It seemed hard to imagine that anyone had it growing in their yard. The few native belladonna species in our area had showy flowers in summer. They were still nightshades, but not nearly as deadly as the Atropa belladonna.

A black and white cat sat up on the braided welcome mat. He stretched and purred and lifted his head for a nice scratch behind the ears. I was happy to oblige. It seemed the cat, too, could rest a little easier now.

I knocked on the door. A few seconds later fingers curled around the lace curtain hanging in the front door window. Marge stared at me a few seconds.

I waved and smiled. "Hello, it's me, Scottie Ramone. The

baker," I added. Most people recognized me easier when I was wearing an apron. She released the curtain and opened the door.

"Hello, I didn't expect to see you here." Marge had her gray hair cut into a bob. She was wearing a thick, hand-knitted sweater that was decorated with chickens. Her blue eyes twinkled. "I don't get many visitors. Would you like some apple cinnamon tea? I've just put the kettle on."

"Tea would be lovely." The cat and I followed her through to the kitchen. It wasn't as fancy and filled with cutesy things as Ingrid's house, but it was still cozy. There was a large framed photo of Marge and her late husband hanging over a carved wooden mantel. They were dressed in holiday sweaters and wearing big smiles.

"That's a great photo over the fireplace," I said.

"Thank you. I love it, too, and whenever I miss Maurice, I stare at the photo for a while and think about all the good memories. It helps." She walked to the cupboard, pulled down another cup and dropped a tea bag inside. "I have some delicious maple cookies."

Just the mention of maple brought my stomach up to an uncomfortable position. "No, thank you. The tea is fine."

She laughed lightly. "I suppose it's rather silly of me to offer cookies to a master baker like yourself."

"That's nice of you to say."

Marge set the cup of tea in front of me and sat down across the table. "I still can't believe what happened at the pie eating contest."

"That's what I was hoping to talk to you about," I said.

Marge looked slightly taken aback. "Me? I wasn't friends with Emery. We were neighbors, but that's all."

"Hannah has mentioned that the two of you were at odds

A Pie For A Pie

over his dog scaring your hens."

"Yes, my poor darlings." As she said it, her cat jumped into her lap. She smiled and gave him a squeeze. "You're my darling, too, Jojo."

"I suppose the hens and the cat are having a much more relaxed day without the big dog next door."

Marge tilted her head in question. "How did you know the dog was gone?"

"Hannah came by for pancakes this morning."

"I see. Yes, Hannah does love your grandmother's company. June picked up the dog yesterday. She wasn't planning to keep him. I feel bad for the dog. He really loved Emery. June mentioned that Emery's business partner was planning to take the dog."

"Do you think June will be moving into Emery's place?"

"Gosh, I hadn't thought of that. This is terrible to say, but it's been such a relief not to have that dog out there, menacing my hens. He jumped over all the time. I'd taken to running my hose and sprinkler so much, the fence posts have started to rot. And do you know Emery had the nerve to complain about that. He told me I had to pay for new fence posts. I told him I wouldn't need to run the sprinkler along the fence if he would keep his dog in the yard."

"I don't blame you for being angry. It sure sounds like Emery wasn't a great neighbor."

"No, he wasn't." Marge's hand flew to her mouth. "That's awful to say now that—well—now that he's gone."

"Yes, but if it's the truth—"

"Oh, it's the truth all right. I can already sense the difference in my hens since June took the dog home."

"That's good. Did you happen to stay for the pie contest? I

thought I saw you at the park before it began. Did you witness the—well—the horrible tragedy?"

Marge was shaking her head as she blew into her tea. "I was there in the morning for a walk, but frankly, I can't stand to watch that contest. It's so messy, and it makes me not want to eat pie…ever. I left before it started. Poor man. Is it true he just keeled over dead?"

"Yes, it's true. It was quite a shock. So, you went home after your walk?"

Marge lifted a brow in suspicion. I'd asked one question too many. "I did. I wasn't at the park long." She sipped some tea. "I heard he died of a heart attack, but your visit makes me wonder if there was something more to it."

"Uh, no, I guess I'm just curious about the whole thing."

"You made the pies for the contest," she stated but tried to make it sound like a question.

I wished people would stop reminding me about that unfortunate fact. "I made the pies."

"Oh well, I'm sure the pie had nothing to do with Emery's death. June mentioned he had a bad heart. Doesn't surprise me. He barbecued himself big steaks every weekend. Didn't seem the least bit concerned about his health or the fact that he'd already suffered one heart attack."

"I guess none of us ever know when our time is up."

"That's right. My poor Maurice started feeling funny one day, and the next thing I knew he was in the hospital trying to fight off an infection. Died three days later."

That answered my next question about how her husband died. I wanted to make sure it wasn't a pattern or something she'd tried before. I had to admit, even though Marge had good motive, she didn't seem like a killer.

"Do you know anything about plants?" I finished my last drop of tea. "In particular, belladonna plants." It was a far-out-of-left-field question to end our chat, but I wanted to see her reaction when I brought up the plant.

She had a very nonreaction—reaction. "Belladonna? Only that it's highly toxic. I keep all those deadly nightshades out of my yard. Even tomato plants can be toxic to chickens. Why do you ask?"

"I heard someone talking about it growing wild in the mountains and that it needed to be avoided. I don't know why I brought it up." I stood and picked up my teacup to carry it to the sink. "Your view is fantastic. I always forget what a wonderful area this is. I'll bet properties don't come up for sale often on Meadowlark Lane."

She was smiling ear-to-ear. "They sure don't. I suppose June won't have any trouble getting top dollar for Emery's place. I only hope she sells it to someone who is allergic to dogs."

nineteen

...

MARGE HAD MOTIVE, she'd been at the park in the morning while Ingrid was still setting up, so she had proximity and her life had now improved because of Emery's death. Still, it was hard to consider her a suspect. She was a sweet, elderly lady who was enamored with her beautiful hens. I had to keep an open mind, but I was moving on to the next suspect on my list.

Thomas Anderson owned a feed store down the hill. Since I was already halfway there, I got in the car and headed toward his store. Mountain Feed and Grain was nestled amongst some tall pines. The shop itself was a square red building with white trim. The hay and straw and large bags of feed were stored in a big red metal building next to the shop. Thomas was having a sale on mucking forks and shovels. They were lined up neatly along the front of the store. A pallet of pine shavings for animal pens sat on the opposite side of the front door. The smell of pine from the shavings and the trees caused me to sneeze on my way in the door.

A Pie For A Pie

"Bless you," someone called from the counter. It was Thomas. He was wearing a green flannel shirt and a green trucker's cap with his store logo embroidered across the crown. He smiled when he saw me. "I don't usually see the town baker in my feed store. Your grandmother comes in all the time to buy birdseed. Is that why you're here? I got in a new mix that has cracked corn and peanuts. I know Evie doesn't like to leave the squirrels out."

I now had my reason for being in the store. I just needed to make a smooth transition to the pie contest. I assumed that wouldn't be hard considering Thomas was right there, just a foot away from Emery when he died.

"Great, I'll take one bag. I'm sure the squirrels will be happy." I followed Thomas past a display of treats for goats, sheep and horses. They were quite fragrant. "Do I smell licorice?" I asked.

Thomas laughed. "That'll be the goat treats. I always carry lots of treats at this time of year because there's very little to forage once the ground freezes." He lifted a big bag of birdseed onto his shoulder. "Just the one?"

"Yes, that'll do for now." I had no idea what Nana's birdseed inventory looked like at the moment, but she probably wouldn't mind an extra bag. I followed him back to the counter. "How are you doing—you know—after yesterday?"

Thomas dropped the bag on the counter with a plunk. He clucked his tongue and added in a head shake. "Can't believe that happened. I wanted badly to win but not like that. It's a hollow victory when your main competitor dies."

"I know you two were trading barbs before the contest, but I assume you were friends. You certainly had that pie contest in common."

"We didn't have much else in common." Thomas lifted his cap and rubbed his forehead before lowering it back down.

London Lovett

"And to be honest, we weren't friends. I've been running this place for twenty years. A big part of my income used to come from renting out tractors and heavy machinery to the locals. Emery and Doug started that excavation business, and they decided to rent some of their equipment, too. My business dried up. The feed store is still doing well, but my profits were cut in half."

"Ouch. That's not good. I can see why you weren't friends."

"I hear it was a heart attack. I suppose that makes sense. Everyone knew about Emery's heart attack a few years back. He was in town when it happened. I think he was just leaving the coffee shop or something like that. Collapsed right there on the sidewalk."

"I wasn't living here at that time, but I heard about his bad heart."

A young woman in a black sweater, jeans and cowboy boots came out from the back room. "Break over already?" Thomas asked. He glanced at the clock on the wall. "Day's going fast. Brenda, could you bring some of that chicken scratch out from the storeroom? I left a space for it on the shelf next to the birdseed."

Brenda hurried off to get the scratch.

"Has Ranger Braddock been in to see you?" I asked as he wrote up a ticket for the birdseed.

"Ranger Braddock? Not yet. I guess he'll probably be in sometime today. After all, I was right next to Emery when he died. Not that I have any details to add. I'm ashamed to admit that I was too busy gloating about my win to notice that something wasn't right with Emery. After I finished the last bite of pie, I glanced over at him to see if he was close to finishing. But he seemed to be just face-down in that pie tin. I hardly saw his jaw or chin moving. It was like he fell asleep in it. I was stunned to say the least. I guess I know why now."

"What time did you get to the park?" I asked.

Thomas arched a thick brow. "About a half hour before the contest. You saw me walking around the lake."

"That's right, I did."

"If I didn't know any better, I'd think you were fishing for my alibi. Is Ranger Braddock going to be asking that, too? Is there more to this than a heart attack?"

I shrugged lightly. "Could be."

"I sure thought something was wrong with his pie. It looked watery, and the cream had dissolved into a mess on top of it. I figured Emery was trying to cheat. I thought he'd tampered with the pie."

"Tampered with it how?"

"Like I say—it looked soupy compared to the rest. I thought maybe he took out some pie and replaced it with water or something to make it easier to finish off quickly. That's why I complained before Ingrid blew the whistle. I guess maybe there was something wrong with that pie after all." He squinted an eye at me, and I knew exactly what was coming next. "Didn't you bake those pies?"

"Yes, you know I did, but all the pies left my shop as perfectly normal pumpkin pies."

"And mine was delicious. Not that I had time to savor or really enjoy it, but it tasted good going down."

"Thank you. Only I'm not sure many people will be coming into my shop for pies this holiday season."

"That's a shame," Thomas handed me my receipt. I was running out of reason to be in the store, and I didn't want to leave without knowing what Thomas had been up to prior to his supposed arrival at the park.

Brenda returned with a rolling cart piled high with chicken scratch.

Thomas reached for the bag of birdseed. "I'll help you out with that," he said.

"No, it's fine. It's not nearly as heavy as sacks of bread flour." I placed my hand on the birdseed and looked up at him. "Thomas, I need to find out what happened to Emery, so I'm just going to ask you point-blank. Where were you yesterday morning, in the hour or so before the contest?"

"Like I said, I was at the park. I strolled right past you."

I tilted my head at him. "Before that?"

"I was right here in the shop setting up that display of livestock treats. I got here around seven. Brenda came in around eight and then I took off a half hour later. Brenda, isn't that right? I was here yesterday morning setting up the treat display."

Brenda looked up from her task a moment. "That's right."

Thomas grinned smugly at me. "Is that all you need to know?"

"Yes, that's it."

"I suppose I'll be answering the same questions from Ranger Braddock."

I smiled sheepishly at him.

"Maybe you two should work as partners. It'd save us all some time."

I forced a chuckle. "Yes, maybe we should." I reached for the birdseed.

"If you want to take a look under-the-hood at someone, you should talk to Doug Hermann, Emery's business partner. His foreman, Mike, comes in all the time to buy alfalfa pellets for his horses. He told me Emery and Doug were in a battle over expansion of the business. Doug wanted to open another branch down in the city, but Emery was being stubborn and cheap about it. He refused to expand. That's who Ranger Braddock and his *partner* should be talking to." He winked at me.

"Interesting. Thanks for the information." I picked up the birdseed and walked out. It seemed I'd found a new fork in the road. Emery had plenty of turmoil in his life. Or was Thomas just trying to throw me off? His alibi was weak at best, and he had more than a contest for motive. It seemed Emery and his company had taken a big chunk out of his feed store profits. I wondered if Dalton knew about the problems at the excavating company. If not, I just moved ahead of him on the gameboard.

twenty
· · ·

I DROPPED the bag of birdseed on the backseat. A few clouds had rolled in to blot out the trickle of warmth the sun was doling out. I got in the car and turned on the heater. The temperature in the mountains could drop precipitously in a matter of minutes. If those clouds decided to drop some precipitation, it seemed we'd have our first snow of the season.

My phone rang. It was Cade.

"Hello, Mr. Toad. You know, 'Frog and Toad' books used to be my favorite. I had all of them. What's up?"

"I made egg salad. My house smells, but I tasted a spoonful, and it's remarkably good. Are you sure I can't lure you my way for lunch?"

"Actually, I've had a lot of sugar this morning, and my body could use a dose of real food. I'm about twenty minutes away. Will that work?"

"I'll be here."

"See you soon." I hung up and noticed I was wearing a big

smile when I glanced in the rearview mirror. I was relieved we were talking again. The one person I hadn't heard from yet this morning was Dalton. He'd been nice enough to fill me in on the preliminary autopsy report, but that seemed to be the end of the information nuggets he was tossing my way. I wondered how far he'd gotten on the case.

I drove up the gravel drive to the Gramby Estate. It looked so much more charming knowing my handsome, smart and successful boyfriend was inside it. It was nice to have him home. There were some weeks when I'd convinced myself I'd never see him again.

Cade came to the door in a sage green sweater and jeans. He was, to put it mildly, breathtaking. At least he'd stolen *my* breath. I was also keenly aware that I looked less than breathtaking. I'd thrown on faded jeans and an old sweater for my investigation. My mind had been on clearing the name of my bakery and not on hair and makeup this morning.

I reached the door and was instantly overwhelmed by men's cologne. I loved the smell of Cade's cologne, but this made my eyes water.

Cade saw me blinking to remove the tears. He laughed. "Then my suspicions are confirmed. Deciding the aroma of egg salad wasn't the best for a romantic lunch, I decided to mask it by splashing on cologne. I might have gone past the splash stage and into the tidal wave stage."

I sneezed and blinked again. "Might have been a touch too much cologne."

"Well, you've got a coat on. I'll get mine, and we can eat on the patio." Cade motioned me inside. "It's even worse in here where the smell of my cologne and the egg salad come together in a calamitous mix that even I, as a somewhat skilled writer, cannot describe."

He was right.

"I think you would have been safer with the egg salad odor. Still, kudos to you for trying to create a romantic lunch." I picked up a plate with a sandwich. "I think the back patio will work, only you'll have to sit at the far end of the yard."

"I'll go change." Cade paused before heading upstairs. "You'll have to excuse me. I'm tragically out of practice with this whole dating thing. Months ago, I would have just let you in, egg smell and all."

I smiled. "I think we can find a nice compromise by staying exactly the way we were but with a little more flirtation and a lot more kissing."

Cade nodded. "Good plan. I'll meet you on the patio, and I'll leave the trail of cologne inside."

I sat out at the patio table. It was chilly for an outdoor lunch, but the view from Cade's patio was amazing. It really was a beautiful property. Cade returned shortly after, smelling much less like cologne.

He was wearing a gunmetal gray sweater that had black stripes around the chest. He held out his arms. "Better?"

"Better. I'll be able to taste my egg salad."

He sat down at the table and waited for me to take a bite.

"Now I know how food critics feel," I said. "It's delicious. Couldn't have done better myself. Although you need to come to the bakery tomorrow for some real bread. This store-bought loaf leaves a lot to be desired."

"I agree. And after Paris, I'm a bread snob. Do you know you can buy a baguette at the petrol station?"

"I lived there," I reminded him.

"Oh, that's right. What a fool I am bragging away about my

time in Paris when you practically grew up there."

"I'd hardly call my three-year stint in culinary school growing up in the place. But I did learn to bake delicious bread in Paris." It seemed we were talking about anything and everything except our new decision to be a couple. I didn't mind. It had been a trying twenty-four hours, and I was all right just shooting the breeze and nibbling sandwiches.

"How is the investigation going? Will your pumpkin pie soon be behind bars?"

"I sure hope not, but even if it manages to escape the long arm of the law, I fear the reputation of my pumpkin pies has been forever scarred. And that's particularly bad considering we're a week from Thanksgiving—the holiday that literally celebrates the pumpkin pie."

Cade rubbed his chin. There was just enough beard stubble there to give him that dark, rugged look. "Isn't Thanksgiving celebrating the early settlers' fortitude? You know Pilgrims and all that."

"Well, yes, if you're going to get literal, but the pumpkin pie was the star of their feast, and that tradition has carried through to modern day."

"I think you might have missed the whole chapter on the colonies when you were in school."

I smiled and took a bite of sandwich. It was nice to have something savory after my morning of maple syrup and brown sugar, two sweet things I adored but not in such quick succession.

"You never answered—" Cade said after a few moments of silent eating. "Have you caught the killer? If not, please allow me to jump in and save the day like last time. I did enjoy being the hero."

"No killer, so I'm afraid I've left my damsel hat behind for now. Emery Gladstone, the victim, seemed to have more than a few enemies. There's his sweet little neighbor and her herd of chickens—"

"I believe the word is flock." He looked at me. "Exactly where did you go to school?"

I waved off the sarcasm. "Marge Bivens had been fighting with her neighbor, Emery. He allowed his big dog to jump the fence between their yards and scare her chickens."

"Well, that's one heck of a motive. So, I'm trying to connect the dots, but I have a lot of floating dots right now. The man died after he ate your pie? Did he choke?"

"Dalton says the pie was laced with poison from the belladonna plant."

"Ah yes, the belladonna plant. I've used that in one of my novels. This is the wrong climate for Atropa belladonna. That's the most dangerous variety. Maybe Ranger Braddock is wrong."

I stared at him for a second. "You just couldn't wait for a chance to say that, could you?"

"Nope. And that was easy, too—didn't even have to work at it. Like I said—wrong climate. Atropa belladonna likes a warm, humid climate."

"Yes, I know all about the plant and its affinity for a tropical climate. And as I'm sure you know, only you ignored it in your quest to say something negative about the ranger, the Atropa belladonna was discovered by the lab. Not the ranger. It was in my pie and in the victim's blood."

"Interesting. Someone went through a good deal of trouble to kill Mr. Gladstone. I assume you're on Braddock's suspect list?"

I wiped my mouth. "You know what? Let's talk about something else."

Cade nodded. "I'd much rather talk about us."

"Me too." I could feel my cheeks warm with the way he looked at me.

"What do you think, Ramone? Can we make this work?"

"As long as your toady side doesn't make too many appearances, I think we can." I reached over, and he took my hand. "I'm not embarrassed to admit I feel like a giddy schoolgirl right now. It's been a long time since I started a new relationship, so I'm a little out of practice."

"Then we'll learn together. But I'll do the teaching because you have some rather large discrepancies in your education."

I laughed as he lifted my hand and kissed the back of it.

twenty-one
...

I LEFT Cade's feeling lightheaded with joy. We'd sat on a cold patio, eating egg salad sandwiches and chatting about silly stuff like school assemblies and how best to eat an Oreo and every second of it was amazing. It was hard to refocus on the serious, far less blissful portion of my day, but I had to find out what happened to Emery. I had a list of suspects, some with good motives and some with flimsy alibis, and something told me that the more I learned about Emery Gladstone, the longer the list would grow.

Nana left a note that she'd gone into town to have coffee with Regina. I had the house to myself, so I decided to chart out what I knew. Sometimes seeing it in graphic form helped pull my thoughts together, and since my thoughts had been further scrambled by my dizzying lunch with Cade, I really needed to set them down on paper.

I pulled a piece of Nana's drawing paper off her pad, grabbed one of her many sketch pencils and sat at the kitchen table. I stared at the blank paper a moment and decided one of Nana's oatmeal cookies would go brilliantly with a brainstorming session. I sat again and stared at the paper. It was nearly impossible not to think about Cade as I stared at the blank paper. He'd kissed me "properly," as he'd called it, before I left, and he'd transferred some of his cologne to my sweater. I lifted the collar of my sweater and took a deep whiff. It was very nice cologne.

I gave myself a shake. "All right, Scottie, snap out of it. Focus." Naturally, for that, I needed a bite of cookie. I ate the bite and decided a glass of cold milk was a necessity. I got up and poured the milk, then sat back down.

"Enough procrastination. This is not long division homework. Stop thinking about the boy and get to work. Your pumpkin pie's reputation has been maligned." I picked up the pencil, and before I wrote down my list of suspects, I allowed the pencil to doodle out the name Cade Rafferty in that fancy, girlie script I used to cover my notebooks with. Only back then it was a different name. And that reminded me, with a rather cold splash of reality, that Dalton might still be focused on Jack. Which meant I needed to get to work.

I wrote Emery Gladstone in a circle in the middle of the paper. No more girlie script. I saved that for boys' names. "Died after eating poison-laced pie," I wrote in the circle. I drew a line and another circle with the name June Greene in the middle. Her motive had started thin. June wanted to get married, but Emery seemed reluctant to make the commitment. I'd also learned that June inherited Emery's valuable property on Meadowlark Lane. It seemed like a long stretch to go from wanting to marry someone to killing them for an inheritance, but maybe June thought if she couldn't have one, she'd have the other. June was not at the pie eating contest, but that didn't mean she wasn't there earlier. I still needed to talk to her and find out why she wasn't at the contest and where she was before it started. With the poison prepared, it wouldn't have taken much time at all to tamper with the pie and make sure the one with the X was placed behind Emery's nametag.

I wrote Thomas Anderson in the next circle. Thomas had been at the park just before the contest. It seemed he had somewhat of an alibi for the earlier part of the morning, the crucial time when the pie was poisoned. But his coworker, Brenda, arrived just before he left for the contest. What if he'd set up the display, raced to the park to tamper with the pie and then hurried back to his shop to set up a convenient alibi with Brenda. It seemed like a stretch, but I kept the option open. While the pie contest seemed like a silly motive, Thomas had taken a big financial hit to his business when Emery's excavation company started renting equipment. But why only Emery? Afterall, Emery had a partner.

And that brought me to Emery's partner, Doug Hermann. It seemed Doug wanted to expand the company, but his aspirations had been thwarted by his partner, Emery. Doug Hermann always looked like the serious and financial partner in the business. I never saw him in anything but a crisp white, button-down shirt and pressed trousers. He was a nice-looking man in his early forties. I rarely saw him in town, and I certainly didn't remember seeing him at the park yesterday morning. Of course, I wasn't looking either. It seemed that there was a far easier way to get your business plans moving forward than murder, but if Emery was dead set against expansion, maybe Doug thought he had no choice. And now Doug Hermann would have the entire company to himself, so all the profits went his direction, and he could expand all he wanted.

My fourth circle was dedicated to Marge Bivens. She had motive. Her neighbor had made her life miserable. She was in a constant battle with Emery to keep his dog on his side of the fence and away from her chickens. Now that problem was solved. Marge also freely admitted she was at the park in the morning before the contest. She left before it started. Was that because she knew the calamity that would follow?

I sat back, nibbled my cookie and admired my chart. If only one of the circles would start blinking with the words "I did it."

I wondered if there were other suspects, future circles to be drawn. I was slowly learning more about Emery Gladstone's life, and it was possible I'd find more suspects. I needed to learn more about his business. The front door opened.

"Button, I'm home." Nana hurried into the kitchen looking flushed and excited. "I was with Regina, and that woman is a veritable treasure trove of gossip and mostly useless information. Of course, we spoke about the terrible tragedy and Emery Gladstone's untimely death. She told me that the Gladstone and Hermann Excavation Company had been having all sorts of legal troubles. They'd been hiring a lot of unskilled machine operators because they could pay them less than the licensed ones."

"That explains my little mishap on the bike the other morning." I realized after I said it that it was a thought better left in my head.

"What mishap? Button, you didn't tell me."

"It's all right. Nothing happened. Please don't fret. One of their trucks dashed by me very closely. It was partially my fault because I wasn't paying attention. The driver was going awfully fast through town. It was fine. But go on. What were you saying about Emery's company?"

Nana got over her moment of angst and took a deep breath. "Well, just what I said—the company has had some lawsuits and complaints about their work."

My phone rang. I wanted to hear more about it, but it was Jack. "Hello, Jack, having a nice day off?"

"I was until Ranger Braddock called to let me know I needed to go to the station for a formal interview."

"What? That's impossible. Dalton is wasting his time. I've got an entire chart of possible suspects, each with a motive to kill Emery. And something tells me there are even more suspects out there."

"Well, he's focused on one and that's me. I've already spoken with him once, but he seems determined to pin this on me." Jack sounded so despondent, I wanted to reach through the phone and hug him.

"I'll meet you at the station. If he's going to interview you, then he needs to interview me as well. And then I'm going to give him a royal piece of my mind."

"Not sure if that will help or hurt," Jack said.

"Well, I'm not going to sit by and watch this happen. I'll see you soon. And don't worry. I'm going to find the real killer, then Ranger Braddock is going to have more than a little egg on his face."

"No sense in you rushing down here right now. There's no telling how long it will take."

"Then please text me as you're leaving the station, Jack. And don't worry. I've got this." I hung up. "No more cookies for that man."

"I'm sure he's just trying to do a thorough job."

"Don't always side with him, Nana. He's wrong about this,

and he needs to know it."

"It'll all work out in the end." It was Nana's go-to line when I was upset about something. I planned to make sure her prediction came true. I was going to find the real killer. I got a text. It was from Esme.

"Just thought I'd let you know that Deidre is in the shop. She's reading a book, and Earl has curled up in her lap, so she'll probably be here for a while. Earl doesn't like to be woken."

"Thanks for letting me know. I'm heading that way now." I folded my chart and stuck it in my pocket.

"Are you leaving?" Nana asked.

"Yep, I've got a witness to interview." I kissed her cheek to hopefully wipe away the earlier terse words. "Wish me luck."

"Oh, Button, you know I always wish you luck."

twenty-two
. . .

MY TEMPER HAD COOLED some by the time I parked in front of the bookshop. I debated whether or not I was overreacting, but I'd fallen firmly on the side of *no*. Since there was only one tainted pie in the bunch, then it followed that the pie was tampered with long after it left the bakery. Jack had no motive to kill Emery Gladstone, and the only reason Dalton was focused on him was because of Jack's prior record. That was unfair. And I intended to let Dalton know just how upset I was about all of this. But first, with the help of some of Nana's perpetual sprinkle of luck, Deidre could add something to the morning that would help me find the real killer.

Like me, Diedre Strong had grown up in Ripple Creek. She worked summers in Roxi's market but was now earning an online degree in hospitality. She had dreams of opening a bed and breakfast somewhere on the mountain. She was sitting in the middle of one of Esme's soft, worn reading couches, and as Esme mentioned, Earl, her fat gray tabby, was curled up in

Diedre's lap. She held her book up over him at a somewhat awkward angle so as not to wake the cat.

Esme poked her head out from one of the book aisles. "How's it going?" she asked.

It would have been strange for me to head straight over to the couch. I knew Diedre but not well. I headed in Esme's direction. She had stacks of books in the aisle as she rearranged her shelves to accommodate the newest inventory.

Esme lowered her voice. "What's going on with the pie contest death?"

I shook my head. "I'm still working on it, turning over as many leaves as possible." I motioned toward Deidre. "In the meantime, the man who is supposed to be turning over those same leaves is focused on one person. Jack. And Jack is in such distress about it."

Esme frowned. "I'm sorry to hear that. I'm sure Dalton will see that he's focused on the wrong person soon enough."

"I think I'll go over and start a conversation with Diedre about the contest. She was right in the heart of it all. Maybe she saw something that seemed out of place." I considered pausing near the couch to look at a few books to pretend as if I just happened by, but my sense of urgency on the matter had increased tenfold. I needed details, and I hoped Deidre had a few to give.

"Hello, Diedre." Earl heard my voice and lifted his big head. He blinked at me a few times and then returned to his nap.

"Scottie, hello, how are you doing?"

I pointed to the open cushion on the couch. "Mind if I sit? I won't keep you long from your book."

She showed me the title. It was Austen's *Emma*. "I've read it at least half a dozen times, so don't worry about that." She tucked her bookmark into the novel and set it on the coffee table in front of the couch. Earl erupted in a loud purr as she stroked his fur. "What a morning, yesterday. I still haven't recovered from seeing poor Mr. Gladstone fall over dead in front of me." Her cheeks lost some color as she spoke.

"Yes, I'm sorry. I guess you really had a front row seat to all of it." I was pleased that she brought the death up first. It made it much easier to ask questions because the topic had already been peeled open. "Diedre, do you mind if I ask you a few questions about yesterday morning?"

She looked slightly puzzled by my request.

"Emery ate one of my pumpkin pies before he died. There's a possibility that someone tampered with his pie, and that's why he died."

Her eyes widened. "So, the poisoning rumor is true? Poor Emery."

At this point, I was more worried about clearing Jack's name than worried about letting official details loose in the infamous Ripple Creek rumor mill. "It looks as if the pie contained poison. Could you recount your timeline for that morning?"

Earl suddenly tired of the conversation taking place over his drowsy head. He hopped up, stretched and sauntered toward an empty book box. With amazing grace for his big size, he hopped right up and into the box.

Diedre laughed as she watched him. "Gee, was it something I said?"

We both had a short laugh. Then Deidre shifted back into the soft cushions.

"Ingrid mentioned that you arrived at the park after her," I started.

"Yes, she told me I didn't need to be there more than an hour before the contest. By the time I got there, Ingrid had already unloaded the pies and set up the nametags on the table." Diedre rolled her eyes. "She was already so stressed by the time I reached the park, I almost regretted taking the job. Ingrid can get very snippy when she's in a bad mood, and she sure was yesterday morning. I don't think this pie contest was on her list of favorite things. She told me it was a silly tradition, and she always got stuck setting it up. Anyhow, she was sipping her herbal tonic like a fiend all morning. She claims it helps with her nerves, but I'm not too convinced it works."

I needed to refocus Diedre. "What about the pies? Ingrid said they were unattended three times that morning."

"Hmm, let's see. Well, Ingrid took them out of the boxes before I arrived. She had them set out on the tailgate of her truck by the time I reached the park. Then we got busy with other things, so yes, they were sitting there alone for a while. And once again, after Ingrid set them out on the table."

"Do you remember seeing anyone lurking around the truck or the table? Someone who wasn't supposed to be there?"

"Gosh, by that time the park was already starting to fill up with people. It could be that a few people wandered into that area. Ingrid and I were so busy we might have missed seeing someone hanging out." She sighed. "I'm sorry. I can't think of anyone in particular. Like I said, Ingrid was in a harried state about all of it. She had me running around like a hen with her tail on fire. It was all kind of a blur."

"Of course. That makes sense. I'll let you get back to your book. Thanks for talking to me."

"Sure thing. I hope Ranger Braddock figures out who did this."

I nodded. "Me, too." I waved to Esme and headed out the

door. My phone rang as I glanced in the bakery window to make sure everything was all right inside my shop. I pulled out my phone. It was Jack.

"Hey, Jack, are you through with the interview?"

"Sure am. I told him everything I know. I gave him a detailed description about how to make a flaky pie crust, which I think irritated him, but he wanted to know about the part I played in making the pies."

I chuckled. "Maybe I'll go into the same painstaking detail about the filling. How are you feeling now?"

"A little better because I think even Braddock realized I had nothing to tell. And I certainly didn't have motive."

"I'm heading to the station right now."

Jack paused. "Uh, let me just warn you that the fiancée and her expensive handbag were just arriving at the station as I left."

My determined shoulder stance deflated. "Darn. Well, this is too important, so I'll just have to steel myself for a Crystal encounter. I'll see you tomorrow, Jack. Try to enjoy the rest of your day off."

"I will. Let me know if there are any developments."

"Sure will." I hung up and took a deep breath. The last person I needed to see right now was Crystal Miramont, but this couldn't wait.

twenty-three
...

CRYSTAL'S LAND ROVER was still parked out front of the station. I was hoping she'd be gone by the time I arrived. I braced myself for seeing her. We hadn't spoken since the day she came into the bakery to angrily tell me to leave Dalton alone. She'd obviously sensed that Dalton was pulling away from her and from the prospect of marriage, and she'd taken her stress out on me.

The ranger station was a prefab building with three windows and no other embellishments. Inside was even less inviting. A long gray counter cut the building in half. There was a sitting area in the front half. Dalton's tiny office was behind the counter, and the multipurpose room in the back was where he interviewed people.

Crystal's heavy perfume permeated the building. The office door opened as I walked inside. Crystal stepped out carrying a glossy blue purse on her arm. Her bright pink lips turned down when she saw me. "What are you doing here?" Her tone was accusatory, and her voice dripped with hate.

Dalton stepped out of the office quickly to find out who Crystal was talking to. His mouth dropped open. "Scottie, it's you."

Crystal forced a smile, and I knew something mean was coming next. In high school, she was what one might classify as a bully. She had it all, beauty and wealth and everything a teenage girl could ask for, but instead of being humble and aware of just how good she had it, she made other people feel bad for not having it all. We were never friends, and she occasionally made fun of something I was wearing or eating, but our true rivalry hadn't really taken shape until that morning in the bakery when she warned me to stay away from Dalton.

"So, I guess the ex-convict baker wasn't a smart business decision after all. I'd say your bakery has two months, tops. Who'd want to buy baked goods from a place that poisons their pies?"

Dalton's face turned red. "Crystal, that is none of your business."

I'd never heard him talk like that to Crystal and, apparently, she hadn't heard it often either. She rolled her lips in and wriggled haughtily in her skin-tight dress. She couldn't find the words to respond, so she turned her wrath back to me. "Speaking of not having business here—you're not a policeman. You mix sugar and flour together in bowls and roll out cookie dough. Stay out of this case. It has nothing to do with you."

My laugh came out even harsher than I'd planned. "You just told me my assistant was going to jail and my bakery had two months, tops. It seems this case has a lot to do with me." I no longer had the energy or patience to deal with Crystal. I came to the station for one reason. I turned to Dalton. "If you interrogated Jack, then you need to interrogate me. I helped make those pies. In fact, I worked on the filling, so if anyone had a chance to poison a pie, it was me."

That seemed to please Crystal. "Maybe he should put you in jail for murder."

Dalton swept past her and pushed open the gate that separated the front of the room from the back. "Go home, Crystal. I've got work to do."

Crystal practically tipped over on her heels. "Are you planning on interrogating her? I think I'll stick around for that."

"No, you won't," Dalton said dryly. "Go home."

As badly as Crystal would have liked to see me behind bars, she didn't seem to like the idea of me sticking around for a one-on-one with Dalton. She hesitated, but Dalton held the door.

"Fine." She stepped through the gate and turned back to him. "Aren't you going to walk me to the car?"

"I told you, I have work to do. Your car is parked right out front. I'll keep an eye out to make sure you get to it safely." There was enough sarcasm in his tone to cause Crystal's foundation to crease on her forehead.

"Don't forget we have dinner reservations tonight with my parents." Crystal's snobby tone, a tone I'd heard far too often in high school, made me cringe.

"I'm too busy. I'll need to skip the dinner. I'm sure your parents won't mind. The last time we sat down together your dad kept glowering at me over his glass of wine."

"No, you can't cancel." She switched to a sweet, flirty tone and then seemed to remember I was standing there. She turned to me with a look that would make grapes shrivel to raisins right on the vine. "Do you mind? We're having a personal conversation."

Dalton tried to interject but I nodded. "I'll move to the waiting area, so you can continue this important conversation." I smiled and walked the three paces to the waiting area. I sat down on the vinyl chair. Crystal was still glaring at me. I smiled again just to irritate her.

She harrumphed so hard, her expensive purse slid off her arm and landed on the ground. Dalton picked it up for her. She snatched it from his hand and dropped it back on her wrist. "I expect to see you at the dinner. And please wear a tie. Sometimes I think you forget the tie just to annoy my parents."

Dalton shook his head. "I'm not going to make it—tie or not."

"I'll discuss this with you when we don't have Miss Nosy Posy listening in on our personal conversation." Crystal swept around with a dramatic hair flip and marched out of the building.

I looked at Dalton. "You forget the tie on purpose, don't you?"

He chuckled, and that great smile melted some of the anger I'd been feeling. "I hate ties, and if not wearing one means causing Mr. Miramont some aggravation, then all the better." He motioned for me to walk to the back. "I suppose I should make this official with the recorder and all the tedious paperwork that goes with it."

I walked through the gate, and we headed to the back room. Crystal's car was just pulling out of the small parking lot. Her tires chirped as they hit the pavement fast and hard.

"I guess my timing could have been better," I said.

A table sat in the center of the room, and there was a chair on each side of the table. Dalton motioned for me to sit before sitting down across from me. He pulled out his phone and was about to press record, then he shook his head. "This is silly.

Look, Scottie, I talked to Jack, and I'm convinced he had nothing to do with the murder."

I sat back and crossed my arms smugly. "You don't say?"

"I had to do my job. I couldn't just brush him off as a suspect because he works for you."

"But you brushed me off pretty fast," I said.

He fiddled with his phone shyly but didn't press record. "That's because you were the girl who used to give me the cookie from her lunch and who made sure I had the right homework assignments and who lent me pencils. How could I possibly consider you a killer?"

"I'm relieved to hear that Jack has been crossed off the list. I've found a few things out today." I looked at him pointedly. "While you were busy wasting time with Jack."

He gave me a disappointed look.

I held up my hand. "You're right. I'm sorry. That's the last comment about Jack. Nana heard through Ripple Creek's very long, convoluted grapevine that Emery's company was having legal problems. Apparently, in order to broaden their profit margins, they'd been using a lot of unqualified drivers for their equipment. There have been some unhappy clients."

"Yes, there are some lawsuits against the company." Dalton was wearing a smile that bordered on admiration. "You sure do get to the heart of these cases."

"Well, as much as I'd like to pat myself on the back for knowing this about the company, Regina is really the person who deserves all the credit. What do you think about pursuing that line of investigation?"

"Already looking into it. I just need to hear back from the company's lawyer."

"You probably also know that Emery and his partner have

been in a dispute about company expansion."

"I've spoken to Doug Hermann, his partner. He's pretty shaken up about the death. At the same time—"

"Doug is now sole owner of the company."

"Exactly. Anyhow, I'm not going to be calling Jack back in, so you can stop being so mad at me."

I pointed innocently at myself. "Me? Mad? No. I just knew you were wasting time. Jack really is amazing."

Dalton nodded. "Yeah, he's a good guy."

"Well, if that concludes our interview, then I'm off." I stood up.

"Where are you off to now?" He stood as well.

"A good sleuth never shares her plans."

"Scottie," he said in an admonishing tone.

"Don't worry. I'll stay out of trouble, but I need to find out what happened to Emery. I can't let my delicious pumpkin pie take the blame."

twenty-four

. . .

I DROVE AWAY from the station as if I had a next step in my plan, but I wasn't sure which direction to go. I needed to know the names of Emery's unhappy clients, but I wouldn't have access to that information. I had to take the more amateur route and read reviews.

I headed to the park. I hadn't revisited the scene of the crime. I liked to do my own evidence search in these cases. I was sure Dalton gave it a good once over, but the park was a big place, and there were so many shrubs and trees and hiding spots, it would be difficult to do a thorough job in just one morning. I planned to park the car and do a quick search of reviews for the Gladstone and Hermann Excavation Company. Maybe some of their unhappy customers left scathing reviews. Afterward, I'd stroll around the park for an evidence search.

I pulled into the lot. It was a brisk day, so the park was empty except for one person. Emery's girlfriend, June, was standing at the spot where Emery fell dead. She was holding a handkerchief in one hand and a bouquet of flowers in the other. Maybe I'd found a better source of information than online reviews.

As I crossed the park, I reconsidered my previous thought. It seemed June was having a private moment of grief and asking her questions about Emery's business didn't seem appropriate. Then again, I needed to move this investigation forward.

I joined her. Her bouquet was filled with fresh-looking flowers, lilies and roses. "Those are beautiful flowers. Did you have to drive all the way down to the city to buy them?" It was the only thing I came up with to get the conversation started, and it wasn't my finest moment.

June looked at the flowers. "Lilies are my favorite. I love fresh cut flowers. This time of year, I buy flowers from Hector Granger. He's a horticulturist with a massive greenhouse. Grows everything you can think of. I thought it'd be nice to start a small memorial here for Emery." Her voice grew shaky, and she wiped at her eyes.

"That's a nice gesture."

Suddenly her sobs grew louder. "I can't believe this happened."

I patted her shoulder. "You must be in a dreadful state of shock."

She nodded and blew her nose. "I am and I'm such a wretched person. I'm a villain. There's no other word for it."

Was I about to hear a confession? "Why would you say that?"

She shook her head, sobbed a few more times and blew her nose. "I gave poor Emery that stupid ultimatum, and when he brushed off my threat, I yelled at him. I told him he'd wasted my time and that I never wanted to see him again." She sniffled loudly. "Those were my last words to him. Horrible, mean

A Pie For A Pie

words and now I can't take them back or tell him I'm sorry."

It was a confession, but not the one I was hoping for. "You can't dwell on that. Try and think about all the good memories you had together."

"I'm trying to do that." She stooped down and placed the flowers on the ground. It was easy to find the exact spot where Emery died because the impressions left behind by the table feet were still visible. June stood up and took a long, deep breath. "Ranger Braddock told me that Emery's death was suspicious. He says they found poison in his system and in the pie." She looked directly at me.

"My pie was tampered with. It left the bakery as a perfectly normal pumpkin pie. What about possible enemies? Was someone angry at Emery? Someone who might have been pushed to murder?"

June rolled her eyes. "Emery always had people angry at him. I swear I used to tell him that while other people avoided conflict and stress, he thrived on it. Like his poor, sweet neighbor, Marge. She's slightly crazy when it comes to her chickens, but he knew there was a simple solution for keeping his dog in the yard. He just needed to add some wire or extra fencing, but I think he was having too much fun angering her."

"Not one of his better qualities," I noted.

"No, definitely not. I guess I always hoped I could change him once we tied the knot. But that was probably wishful thinking."

"What about with his business? I've heard he had problems with a few clients."

"That was another constant source of tension." June started walking, so I tagged along. She didn't seem to mind. "The company was doing well, well enough to keep both partners flush with money. Then they decided to start renting out equipment, and that turned out to be lucrative."

"Yes, because they took the money away from Thomas Anderson's business."

Without formally planning it, June and I reached the walking path around the lake. Most of the birds had left for the winter, and the usual chorus of frogs had fallen silent with the first whisper of fall. "Thomas came to talk to Doug and Emery about it. He was so mad. He told them it wasn't fair that they stole his rental clients."

"When was this?"

"Gosh, maybe two years ago. That'd be a long time to hold a grudge. However, Thomas did badly want to win that contest." She turned her face toward me. "You don't think—"

"I have no idea. What about the disgruntled clients?"

She laughed lightly. "There were plenty. It was all about profit for Doug and Emery. Doug was even greedier. He'd been pleading with Emery to expand the business, but Emery was sure that would shrink profits too much. They argued about it a lot." She shook her head. "Like I said, Emery thrived on conflict."

"Do you know the name of some of their dissatisfied clients? Someone who badly wanted reparations and didn't get it?"

"There were a few, but I can't remember names. But I know of one man, in particular, because he happens to live next to Hector Granger, where I buy my flowers. The worker was excavating some land, so the owner could build a porch. The big bucket swung too close to the house—it actually hit the building and caused some major damage. I can't remember the man's name, but he filed a lawsuit against the company when Emery and Doug refused to reimburse him or pay for the damage. He had a funny name." She lifted her face in thought. "Wendell or something like that. I guess Ranger Braddock has his work cut out for him. I hope he finds out who did this." Her tone returned to the wavery one from earlier. "Emery might have been stubborn and contentious, but he didn't deserve this."

"I agree. I'm sure Ranger Braddock will find the person. I understand you'll inherit the property."

She hesitated, apparently surprised that I knew that piece of information.

"Rumors shoot around this town at lightning speed," I explained. "So, it's not true?"

"No, it's true. I have no idea what to do with that big parcel of land. I've got my own place, and I'm content there. I'll have to sell it. It's really the last thing I want to deal with at a time like this." We circled around the end of the lake and headed back the way we came. It was late afternoon, and the sun would hide behind the distant peaks in an hour. If I planned to do a search, I needed to start.

"Well, I'm sorry for your loss, June, and I'm sure justice will soon be served."

twenty-five
. . .

JUNE WALKED to her car and drove off. Her pretty bouquet of flowers had already started to soften, the petals withering, by the time I reached the spot where Emery died. I stood still and turned around like a beacon in a lighthouse. It was hard to know which way to walk, and daylight was fading fast. I took off toward the area with the lushest landscape. Half a dozen plump junipers lined a section of the trail. They'd make the perfect hiding place for evidence. I just wasn't sure what kind of evidence I was looking for. There was a strong possibility that this search was a waste of time.

Like parting hair, I moved aside branches to look deeper into the shrubs. I moved along the line of junipers. Nothing. I glanced around. Numerous thin, naturally-worn footpaths led away from the center of the park. The killer could have easily snuck in and out of the pie scene unnoticed. I strolled along at an investigator's pace as I walked each of the paths. As I circled around a spruce tree, my ankle twisted on a fallen pine cone.

"Ouch." I sat on a nearby rock and rubbed my ankle. It wasn't too bad of a twist, and once the initial pain subsided, I was able to step fully on my foot again. As I rounded the rock to continue up the trail, the toe of my shoe struck something beneath the rock. My snake-phobic mind went straight to the notion that I'd just woken a rattlesnake from his cold-weather nap. My body reacted with a surge of adrenaline. I jumped back. It gave me a better view of the rock. Something white was wedged beneath it, and it wasn't a snake (thank goodness).

I walked back to the rock and stooped down. A pair of latex gloves would have been nice to have, but I didn't have any in my pockets so I had to improvise. I searched around for the biggest fallen leaf I could find, a dark yellow maple, and I used it like a tissue to pull free the white object. I recognized it before the yellow bulb emerged from the rock. It was a turkey baster. It was the perfect tool for injecting liquid poison into a pie. I left the baster near the rock and pulled out my phone.

Dalton answered on two rings. "Scottie? What's up?"

"I think I found out how the killer tampered with the pie. Unless someone decided to take their turkey baster for a hike, I've found an important piece of evidence."

Dalton didn't respond.

"Dalton?" I asked. "Are you there?"

"Yeah, I'm here—smacking myself in the head for not finding such a key piece of evidence."

"Don't beat yourself up too badly. It was mostly hidden under a rock, and I came to that rock by clumsily stepping on a pine cone and then finishing that graceful moment with a comical rattlesnake freakout dance. There's a lot of landscape out here—"

"Stop, Scottie. I blew it. I should have found it. Don't touch it.

I'll be there soon." He sounded angry and curt and frustrated. He hung up without another word.

Someone coughed. I walked in that direction. A man with broad shoulders, a jacket with Gladstone and Hermann Excavation written across the back and thick work boots was standing staring down at the flowers June had left. He placed a can of beer next to the flowers.

I didn't want to startle him, so I cleared my throat loudly as I walked out from the surrounding landscape. He glanced in my direction.

"Afternoon." I looked pointedly at the flowers and beer. "I see someone has started a memorial for Mr. Gladstone. I was at the pie contest, and I still can't believe it. I'm Scottie. I own the bakery in town."

The man looked to be about thirty. There was a thin layer of dust on his coat, and the smears on his face assured me there'd been plenty of dust there, too. "Zach, I worked for Mr. Gladstone. He was a good guy. Sometimes he'd bring a twelve pack of beer into the office on Friday afternoon, and all of us would have a cold one together to celebrate the end of a work week."

"I'm sure Mr. Hermann, his partner, is very broken up about it. All of you are, for that matter."

"Yeah, it'll be different at work, that's for sure." Zach lifted his work cap and pushed his hair back before replacing it. "Mr. Hermann says there'll be some changes. He wants to expand the business, and some of us are looking forward to moving down the mountain."

"Yes, I've heard expanding the business was a source of contention between the two owners."

"They always had different visions for the company. Hard to see how they ever became partners in the first place." It seemed

A Pie For A Pie

I'd stumbled not just upon an employee, but one who didn't mind talking about the company.

"June was here earlier. She brought those flowers," I said.

"I figured they were from June. She's got to be heartbroken." He looked at me. "I heard it was the pie. Did you say you owned the bakery?"

I nodded and shrugged. "I assure you I don't bake poisonous pies."

"So, someone poisoned the pie on purpose," he deduced. It was always hard to know how much information people knew, and something told me Zach didn't hang out in circles that were tied into the local gossip.

"That seems to be the case," I said. "Do you mind if I ask you a question?"

"Sure, but it seems that you know more about all this than me."

"Honestly, I'm just trying to clear the name of my bakery. Like I said—my pies are quite delicious and perfectly harmless."

"Unless you count calories," he said with a deep chuckle.

"Fair point. I heard a man was suing the company because of damage to his house."

Zach smiled. "Boy, news does travel fast in this town. It's true, but Mr. Symfield caused the damage himself. He'd rented one of our excavating machines. Insisted he knew how to handle it. But he swung the bucket too close to his house and took off an entire corner. He came back shrieking and yelling and insisting the machine jumped out of his control, but when we tested it, it was fine. It was driver error, and since he signed a waiver—"

"He doesn't have much legal leg to stand on," I said.

The sun was slipping behind the peaks, and the park was

bathed in cold shadows.

Zach zipped up his jacket. "Nah, not really. I haven't heard any updates about the lawsuit. Mr. Hermann hasn't mentioned it. But Mr. Symfield has come to the office more than once ranting and raving and insisting the company pay for the damage. One time I was sure the guy would bust a blood vessel. His face was bright red, and Emery, Mr. Gladstone, he'd just sit there with his arms crossed letting the guy throw his tantrum and then he'd say 'no can do.' It was kind of mean, to be honest. I don't blame the guy for being so upset. I heard a whole corner of his house was demolished. That'd cost a lot of money to fix."

"Poor Mr. Symfield." June only had snippets of the story. In her version it sounded as if one of the company drivers had done the damage, but it seemed Mr. Symfield had taken on a task that was beyond his skills. I needed to speak to Mr. Symfield, and I had to resort to sneakiness to find out where he lived. "Mr. Symfield," I repeated and tapped my chin. "I once baked a birthday cake for a Mr. Symfield. He lived over on—hmm—on—"

"He's out on Rocking Horse Drive."

I snapped my fingers. "That's the man. Wendell Symfield, right?" I had a street, and how hard could it be to find a house with a corner missing? June mentioned that Wendell lived next door to the man who grew flowers in a big greenhouse. That should help, too.

"Yeah, that's him." Zach adjusted his hat. "Well, I've got to head home or the wife will be worried."

"Nice talking to you." There were still a million questions I could ask him, but he'd already given me some good information. I didn't want to push my luck. Now I needed to wait for Ranger Braddock to come pick up the key piece of evidence. I just hoped he wasn't too grumpy about it.

twenty-six
. . .

I SAT on one of the benches at the chess table to wait for Dalton. A phone call interrupted my thoughts where I was formulating my next steps. It was Cade.

"Hello, world famous author," I said.

"Oh please, I'm only semi-famous. I did, however, call to brag that my agent sold the movie rights for my last book."

I sat up in excitement. "That's fantastic. So, we'll be seeing it on the big screen?"

"Only if all the stars line up properly, and the earth tilts just right on its axis and Jupiter is in retrograde. No idea what that means, but I've heard the phrase somewhere. Selling the rights is a first step, but it's still a long journey to an actual movie. I've sold the rights to two of my other novels, and they never made it past the rights being sold. I guess I've got a few more twinkles of hope for this one because it's doing well."

"Still, we should celebrate."

"I'm never one to turn down a celebration. I know this is

your day off. Where are you?"

"I'm at the park waiting for—"

He waited for me to finish, then chuckled. "Guess I can finish that sentence myself."

Dalton's truck pulled into the lot as I looked up. "You know what? You're right. I'm not going to pretend or lie or leave blanks unfilled. I'm waiting for Ranger Braddock. I found a crucial piece of evidence that with any luck and some nice fingerprints might solve the case."

"A crucial piece of evidence? Isn't that his job?"

"It's a big park, and there are a lot of hiding places. I know because when I was a kid, Nana used to organize a big Easter egg hunt for me and all my friends. We'd race through the park in our tall rubber boots and thick gloves and sweep up every egg in the park. Or at least that's what we thought. We'd still be finding those eggs weeks and months later. It was easy because they'd start to smell."

"I'm sorry. I missed most of that because I was picturing all of you in tall rubber boots and thick gloves. We used to have to wear our uncomfortable and hideous Easter Sunday outfits for the hunt. Kudos for originality, Ripple Creek."

"Oh, it wasn't for originality. It was because of the snakes. They were always coming out of hibernation at that time of year."

"I imagine dozens of hardboiled eggs probably woke them up early. See, that's what I love about you, Ramone. The conversation started about Braddock's lack of skills and transitioned quite easily into waking snakes from hibernation."

"Cade, stop that."

"I will. Just give me some time."

"And at the risk of ruining this moment even more, Dalton is here, and I need to show him the new evidence."

"I'm going to hang up now. Celebration later?"

"Yep. Bye." I pushed the phone into my pocket and headed toward Dalton. The look on his face wasn't anger. He looked sad. It was the easiest label I could find for the expression on his face. And it wasn't just his face. His whole body lumbered sluggishly along as if he'd been up all night or forgotten his morning coffee.

We both reached the flower and beer memorial at the same time. "Where is it?" he asked coldly. No greeting or hint of a smile.

"If you're that angry about me finding it first, I could just point you in the right direction and let you know if you're getting colder or hotter." My chiding fell flat. "I'm sorry. Come this way." I led him past the juniper and to the rock where I'd sat to rub my ankle. The turkey baster was sitting on the maple leaf. "I used the leaf to pull it free from the rock. I only touched one spot on the baster, and it was with the leaf as a barrier." I pointed to the crevice beneath the rock. "It was wedged inside there."

Dalton pulled on a pair of gloves. His cheek twitched, a sure sign that he was in a tense mood.

"Would you rather I hadn't found it?" I asked sharply. It seemed I at least deserved a thank you.

"Huh?" He shook his head. "No, I'm glad you found it. Apparently, I need to start looking for a new job, a new town, a new life."

"Uh-oh, someone is feeling down in the dumps. I thought as much when I saw you trudging across the park. The last time I saw you walk that way was when your soccer team was walking off the field after losing the championship game."

The memory put a smile on his face. "At least back then, win or lose, you still got to have pizza and root beer." He stooped down and held up the baster. "I guess we can assume this didn't roll out of someone's kitchen and accidentally land here under the rock. And now we have an important piece to the puzzle. Let's see if the killer was careless enough to leave fingerprints."

"I was hoping that, too." We walked along the trail. "Why so grim this afternoon? I hope it's not because of that turkey baster."

"No, although I'm feeling like a complete failure for missing it."

"It's a big park. I would have missed it, too, if I hadn't tripped on a pine cone."

Dalton glanced over at me with a confused brow.

I waved my hand. "Let's just say it was one of my typical chain of events, only this time it helped me find some evidence. What's going on? I mean with the clumpy footsteps and frown."

"I told Crystal I couldn't make the dinner. You heard me. I was pretty plain about it, but she texted me to let me know I should wear the light blue tie she bought me last month. When she doesn't get her way, she just barrels over me until I relent and do what she asks. When did I become such a marshmallow?"

I looked over at him.

He nodded. "Yeah, you don't need to answer that. It happened the day Crystal and I decided to date, and she's been controlling my life ever since."

We stopped when we reached the flowers. "I don't want to tell you what to do, especially in this case, but it's time to take control of your own life. It's the same advice I'd give anyone. Somewhere, somehow, Dalton, you need to find your way back to yourself."

His hint of a smile gave me some hope that my words had helped.

"Still always the smartest girl in town." Dalton lifted the evidence bag. "And pretty darn handy in a murder investigation, too."

"Oh, speaking of that," I said. "Did you know that a man named Wendell Symfield is suing Emery's company—"

"For damage to his house. Despite looking like a complete Inspector Clouseau on this case, I am on top of a few things."

I laughed. "I'm sorry. I didn't mean to make you feel like Clouseau. Although didn't he always solve the case in his clumsy, convoluted and comical way?"

"A lot of stupid luck on his part, I think. But back to Symfield. The case was already dismissed. Symfield was driving the machine, and he wasn't the least bit qualified to operate the thing. He's angry about it, but he's accepted the judgment. He told me he was painting his bedroom yesterday morning and never went near the park or the pie contest. He lives alone. I checked, and his bedroom was freshly painted. Not that that gives him a solid alibi. He's still on the list."

"But Jack and I? Are we crossed off with permanent marker now that I found that?" I pointed to the baster.

"I'm sure this will test positive for belladonna, and yes, I think that pretty much concludes the part of the investigation where I anger the town's baker and my best friend."

It took a second for me to comprehend what he said. I looked up at him. "Am I your best friend, Dalton?"

"Well, you're a close second after Evie. And I'm thinking about what you said. I'm through with this game Crystal and I are playing. It's not even a game. She's playing it all by herself, and I'm just her pathetic pawn."

A Pie For A Pie

"Dalton, it sounds like you've come to a serious conclusion about your relationship."

"I have and this time no matter how many fits she throws, I'm sticking to my decision. It's not going to change for me. I've already known for months that it's not going to work between us. I just hope her father doesn't pull rank and call his connections to get me fired from my post."

"You don't actually think he'll do that, do you?" I asked.

"He's never liked me, and he'll be thrilled that this is over. At the same time, he'll want to make sure to take me down a few notches."

"Well, the town will come out in full protest if he tries it, and your two best friends will be at the front of the protest." I rubbed my hands together. "Gee, it's getting cold out here." According to my calculations, I had just enough time to drive to Rocking Horse Drive and find Wendell Symfield's three-cornered house.

Dalton walked me to the car. "Are you heading home? Tell Evie hello for me."

"I will." I decided it was best not to mention my last stop before home. I was feeling better that my latest find had taken Jack cleanly off the suspect list, but there was still the matter of clearing my pumpkin pie's good name. I smiled up at Dalton before I got in the car. "Good luck with, you know, well—everything."

"Thanks. I'm going to need it."

twenty-seven
. . .

THERE WAS ONLY a whisper of daylight left as I pulled onto Rocking Horse Drive. The small street was shaped like a horseshoe, but I had no idea if that was how it got its name. I spotted the greenhouse first. It was impressive and took up almost the entire backyard behind a house with gray siding and a stone porch. The house to the right was a small white farmhouse with a white porch that was covered in vines. Wood siding was hanging off in shards on the front corner of the house. A man with tufts of white blond hair and dressed in denim overalls was standing on the side of the house trying to herd some energetic chickens toward a coop. I had no idea what Wendell Symfield looked like, but the man in the overalls looked like a Wendell. I got out of the car and headed toward the side of the house.

Three of the hens made a run for it. I lowered my hands and started corralling them toward the rest of the gang. After a few seconds of zigging and zagging around the yard, we managed to get all the chickens safely in the coop.

A Pie For A Pie

"Thanks for your help. They love leaving the coop, but going back in for the night is always a challenge."

"I think that's how it is for parents of young kids, too," I said with a laugh.

With the chickens safely tucked in bed, it was time for Wendell to ask the obvious question. He glanced toward the street where my car was parked. "Are you lost?"

"Actually, no." The chickens helped break the ice, but now I had to keep the chat going. Telling the truth seemed to be my easiest route. "I'm Scottie Ramone. I own the bakery in Ripple Creek."

"Ah yes, you have a lot of fans. I try to avoid carbohydrates."

"Probably a smart move. You're Wendell Symfield, right?"

His brows lowered in suspicion. "That's right."

"I'm sure you heard about the incident at the pie contest."

"Of course. Emery Gladstone died suddenly after eating the pie." He seemed to be putting all the pieces together. His suspicious brow faded. "And you're trying to find out what happened to Emery so that you don't lose customers?"

"That's exactly right."

He turned and double-checked the gate on the chicken yard. "Ranger Braddock already came to talk to me." I followed him as he walked to the other side of the coop and flicked on a light switch. A warm, red glow filled the interior of the henhouse. "I was having trouble with Gladstone and Hermann. They rented me faulty equipment, and I thought they should have paid for the damage—" He stopped and shook his head. "No longer important. The judge made a decision, and I've accepted it."

"Do you know any other clients who might have a grudge against the company? Was there an online group or something for people with similar issues?"

Wendell turned and shoved his hands into his overall pockets. "I've heard there's been other issues. The company doesn't have great reviews, so I assume there are other people with complaints, but I don't get involved in online chat groups or anything like that." Wendell looked past me. He rolled his eyes briefly and then forced a smile. "Hector, how's it going?"

I turned around. A man in his late fifties or early sixties was walking toward us carrying a bundle of fragrant basil. He looked familiar. I'd seen him in the bakery. "I just pruned my basil plants, and I thought you could use some."

Wendell nodded and took the basil. "Thanks. Looks like I'm making marinara tonight."

Hector nodded politely to me.

"Hector, this is Scottie Ramone. She owns the—"

Hector stuck out his hand. "The bakery. I love your cinnamon rolls. They remind me of the ones my grandmother used to make on Christmas morning."

"I always consider it the greatest compliment to have my baked goods compared to a grandmother's treats. Nice to meet you."

"Ms. Ramone is here because her pumpkin pie was the last thing Emery Gladstone ate." Wendell wasn't wrong, but it was hard not to be irritated by his wry tone.

"I've heard about that," Hector said. "But, of course, his death had nothing to do with your delicious pie. Poor man. Wendell, there were two purposes for my visit. I wanted to deliver the basil, and I wanted to remind you to lock up at night. Saturday night I went out to pick some spearmint for my tea, and I found the door to the greenhouse slightly ajar. I know I closed it tight. I don't want the warm, moist air to get out or the cold night air to get in."

"I'm sure the wind blew it open," Wendell said. It seemed he used the same wry tone for a lot of his conversation.

"No, no, I made sure to shut it properly."

"Was anything taken?" I asked.

"Well, I did a quick inventory on Sunday morning. If they did take something, they took cuttings or small snippets of plants. All they had to do was ask. I don't mind sharing a few herbs, now and then. I don't charge much for any of my plants. I have a lot of customers who are happy to pay me for herbs and flowers."

His mention of flowers reminded me of June. "That's right. I just saw June Greer at the park with the bouquet of flowers she got from your greenhouse. Very nice blooms."

Hector beamed. "Thank you. Although, lately, I've been growing fewer flowers and turning more toward medicinal herbs and plants. People are always looking for more holistic ways to cure what ails them." He smiled at his neighbor, who was, once again rolling his eyes. "Wendell thinks it's all silly mumbo jumbo."

"Never said that, Hector. I just think people shouldn't fall for every cure and tonic they find online. Too many plants are more harmful than helpful."

As he said it, a big, bright lightbulb went off over my head. "Hector, you don't by any chance grow Atropa belladonna?"

Hector nodded. "I do, but it's for scientific reasons. I like to adjust temperatures and humidity and experiment with different combinations of the two. Atropa belladonna is my 'canary in a coal mine,' so to speak. It lets me know when it's too hot or too humid in the house. I'd never sell it. It's far too lethal."

An owl began its nightly chorus of hoots somewhere in the tall evergreen canopy. "That's my cue to go inside and cook that marinara," Wendell said. "Thank you for helping me round up the chickens," he said to me. "And Hector, thanks for the basil." He lifted the bunch, and it released more aroma before he turned and headed inside.

Hector and I walked toward the road. "Do you think someone could have cut some of the belladonna plant without you realizing it?" I asked as we reached the road.

"I suppose so, but I'm not sure why they'd bother. You can't do much of anything with a belladonna plant, and it doesn't grow up here without a greenhouse. But I'll be putting a lock on that greenhouse door in case the thieves return."

"That might be a good idea. You know, I wouldn't mind buying a few herbs."

Hector grinned. "Absolutely. Follow me."

It was getting dark and cold, and I was getting hungry, but my stomach could wait a few minutes. There'd been so much talk about belladonna in the past twenty-four hours, I wanted to see the plant in person.

We walked inside, and I was instantly surrounded with comforting warm, aromatic air. "Wow, that's quite the contrast from the outside temperature," I noted.

Hector laughed. "I love to sit in here with my plants and watch the snow fall outside."

"That does sound wonderful. Uh, before we pick the herbs, which one is the Atropa belladonna?"

"You sure are interested in that one." Another laugh. He led me over to a table that was brimming with lush green, tropical-looking plants. "This right here is the belladonna." The plant certainly didn't look lethal with its lime green, supple leaves and charming little purple bells. A few plants had berries. "These berries are the most poisonous part, right?"

"Yes, but the entire plant is poisonous."

One section of the plant had been clearly trimmed of a few branches. "Looks like someone cut off some branches on this side."

Hector moved to get a better view. He gently lifted the branches. "You know, I think you're right. Looks like a clean cut. Well, I'll be darned. Why would someone do that?"

To poison Emery Gladstone, I thought but didn't say out loud. "Is June Greene a frequent customer?" I asked.

"Sure is. She likes to have fresh flowers in her home." He reached for a pair of cutting shears on the wall. "Now, which herbs are you interested in?"

I'd used the herbs as an excuse to see inside the greenhouse, but now, it seemed, I was going to be making a purchase. I was sure Nana would appreciate a few fresh herbs. "How about some sage, rosemary and thyme," I said.

Hector nodded enthusiastically. "I'll add in some parsley for free. I call it my Simon and Garfunkel special. Coming right up."

twenty-eight
. . .

IT HAD BEEN SUCH a long day; I couldn't wait to get to Cade's and relax with a glass of wine and witty conversation. I promised myself that I wouldn't bring up the murder case. I needed a break from the investigation. This was an evening to celebrate Cade's success. It seemed even he was stunned at how well his latest novel was doing. It was far too dark and cold to consider a walk to Gramby Estate. Not only that, but I'd taken the bold move of wearing some heels with my dress. I figured a celebration called for a nicer wardrobe.

I glanced at my phone before opening the car door. I'd left Dalton a voicemail letting him know I was certain I'd found the source of the poison. He hadn't called or texted. That was fine. It could wait until tomorrow. And with that, I ended the investigation for the evening. I was about to have a drink and quality time with my very handsome, charming new boyfriend, and since the word *boyfriend* had not been in my vocabulary for some time, I was feeling especially giddy.

A Pie For A Pie

Cade came to the door. He was wearing a dove-gray button-down shirt and black trousers. I was glad I'd opted for a dress and heels. "Why, is that Hollywood's next big—" I paused. "Wait, what title do they give writers who contribute their book to a movie?"

"Just that. When the credits roll it will say *Cade Rafferty, writer who contributed his book to the movie.*"

I stepped inside, and he quickly pulled me into his arms for a kiss. I couldn't see my eyes as I smiled up at him, but I was sure they contained gold sparkles. "A girl could get used to this kind of greeting."

"Good." He dipped his head toward me. "As long as I'm on one side of the greeting, and you're the *girl* end of that scenario. I was just about to pop the cork on an expensive bottle of champagne. I figured tonight called for the kind that actually came from France and not the local Booze and Beverage."

"Excuse me, Mr. Continental, but I'm pretty sure they can't label it champagne if it doesn't come from France."

Cade stopped and pursed his mouth. "That must be why the last bottle I bought said Champoone. I thought it was a label error."

I laughed. "All right. End of that silly discussion. Pop that cork, sir. I've got a toast just waiting to break free from this mouth."

Cade's gaze fell to my mouth. "That mouth? The one behind those incredible lips?" He leaned forward and kissed me again. I could feel a blush heating up my entire face, and I hadn't even had a sip of champagne yet.

Cade straightened. His hazel eyes looked green under the kitchen light. "I'm glad you came, Ramone. None of this would mean a thing to me if you weren't standing here."

"I'm glad to be here, and I'm feeling extra proud and braggy about my boyfriend." I sucked in a short breath and stared at him with worry.

"What's wrong?" he asked.

"Is it all right that I call you *my boyfriend*?"

He took my hand and kissed the back of it. "Only if I can call you my *little lady*."

A laugh shot from my mouth. "Little lady?"

"No? All right, then we'll go with the traditional, albeit ordinary, *girlfriend* label."

Cade popped the cork and it was followed by a cascade of bubbles. He turned to hold it over the sink. "Oops, might have gotten a little shaken up in the back of the car."

I carried over the glasses, and he poured us each some champagne.

He put the energetic bottle in the sink to finish its bubble tantrum and turned to me with his glass.

"To Cade and his extreme talent with words and…with my heart." We tapped glasses and took a sip. I wriggled my nose in the effervescence still radiating off the glass. "This, sir, is a very nice champagne. I'm glad you left the Champoone corked for this particular occasion."

We each took another sip, then Cade took the glass from my hand and set both glasses down on the kitchen counter. He pulled me into his arms again. "About that toast—I rather liked it."

He leaned forward for a kiss. My phone rang right then to disrupt the lovely moment. I never ignored a phone call in case it was Nana, and Cade knew that. He lowered his arms. "Hold that thought and that kiss," I said as I pulled out my phone. It wasn't Nana. It was Dalton. I looked up at Cade, and he rolled his eyes.

"Just answer it. I'll get the cheese tray out of the fridge." His broad shoulders looked mildly tense as he turned to walk to the fridge.

"Hello, Dalton, I can't—"

"I did it," he blurted before I could let him know I was too busy to talk. "I told her we were through, and, of course, she threw a fit and cried and told me I was the worst person in the world. I hung up during her tirade." Dalton was on a full rush of adrenaline, and he was talking so fast I couldn't get in a word. "Then her father called to let me know I was through up here on the mountain and that I might as well move to Timbuktu because I was never going to find a job again if he had anything to do with it."

I smiled sheepishly at Cade as he walked past with the cheese tray. He didn't look my direction.

Dalton finally paused to catch his breath.

"I'm sure his threats are hollow." Of course, I had no idea if that was true or not. Mr. Miramont had a lot of money and power. I hated to think that he could get Dalton fired, but I imagined it was possible. "It sounds as if you're relieved to be past this, Dalton, and I hope that this will be the change you need to move on with your life."

"It is and I have you to thank for that."

"Wait, you didn't say that to Crystal, did you?" Had I stuck my neck out too far on this? I only wanted to help Dalton get past all the troubles that were weighing him down.

"No, of course not, Scottie. By the way, this evening has been a bit of a blur, but you left a voicemail—something about finding the source of the poison."

"Yes, but that can wait." I could see through to Cade's living room. He looked glum and bored and amazingly handsome considering he was glum and bored. "I'll talk to you in the morning, Dalton. I need an evening away from the case."

His phone beeped. "Oh boy, that's probably Crystal's mom. She hasn't called me yet to let me know what a horrible, awful person I am. I think I'll ignore it and go home and celebrate with a beer. Talk to you tomorrow, Scottie."

I was relieved that the call ended quickly. I walked shyly and slowly into the living room. Cade was eating a chunk of brie on a cracker.

"Am I invited to the cheese party?" I asked. "I promise I won't answer any more calls unless it's Nana."

He didn't answer at first.

"Cade, you said you'd try harder."

He sighed. "I did. But he doesn't make it easy."

I sat on the couch next to him. "It's only because there's a murder case happening. I promise this will get smoother." I leaned forward and pushed some brie on a cracker. I turned to him before eating it. "Okay, *boyfriend*?"

I leaned against him, and he put his arm around my shoulder. "You're a hard person to say no to, Ramone."

twenty-nine

. . .

JACK and I had returned to work and spent our usual early morning in a tornado of flour, powdered sugar and baking powder. We watched the sun come up and slowly send its light and warmth through the front window of the shop. Brownies were frosted, pastries were glazed and freshly baked bread was in the baskets waiting to be plucked up, sliced and sent home in brown bags. Only the customers didn't come. We had a few of our morning regulars pass through, but there was no denying it—Emery's death had hurt business. I stood behind the counter wiping it down for the tenth time. Jack came out from the back after taking a phone call.

"That's another holiday pie cancellation," he said glumly. "People are so ridiculous."

I tilted my head his direction. "Well, a man did drop dead after eating one of our pies." The hard work had helped push the case out of my head for the morning, but standing in my extremely deserted bakery, it was back, front and center. "Jack, I need to go talk to Emery's business partner, Doug Hermann. He has motive. Emery's death leaves Doug as the sole owner of the business."

"So his wealth just doubled," Jack pointed out.

"Exactly, and he can now make his own decisions about which way to move the company. Apparently, he'd been wanting to expand, and Emery had been his only obstacle. Now that obstacle is gone."

"I can watch the shop." He glanced around at the empty space. The glass cases were brimming with goodies just waiting to be placed in pink boxes. "Wow, we've really taken a hit with this. I can't believe it."

"I'm determined to make this our only slow day." I untied my apron. "If you don't mind captaining the ship—" My attention was pulled to the front window as several people looked inside, frowned and then continued walking. "If you don't mind captaining the *ghost* ship for a bit, I'm going to head out into the cruel world and clear our good name."

"Aye, aye." He saluted me.

I grabbed my keys and headed to the car.

Gladstone and Hermann Excavation was located a good five miles down the mountainside. The company consisted of three mint green Quonset huts and four vast yards where the big machines were stored. The entire lot was a mix of loose gravel and dirt. It wasn't fancy or modern, but I was sure the company turned over an impressive profit. I pulled in next to some work trucks. I'd seen Doug Hermann a few times. He and his wife came in to order a birthday cake for their daughter in summer. While Emery had been the big, burly, faded-flannel-and-jeans side of the company, Doug was the clean fingernails, aftershave, business-suit side of it. He was sitting behind a large metal desk inside the main hut. There were metal file cabinets lining both sides of the building, and a portable heater was making a loud noise in the corner.

He glanced up from his paperwork. "Morning. The rental office is next door."

"I'm not here about a rental," I said.

"Great, if you're interested in hiring our company, I have to warn you we are booked until next February. Is this a new house or a landscaping job?" Nothing about the man's demeanor said he was grieving the loss of his partner. I saw far more emotion from Zach, the man who worked for them.

I sat in the seat in front of the desk. "It's neither."

He scrutinized my face a second. "Wait, aren't you the baker from up in Ripple Creek?"

"Yes, that's me. I'm Scottie Ramone."

"Trina loved her birthday cake, by the way."

I smiled. "I'm glad to hear it. Unfortunately, the fate of my bakery is unknown now because of your partner's death."

It was the first glimmer of grief I'd seen so far. But was it fake? His mouth turned down, and his face dropped with it. "Yes, it's been a shock to everyone. I still keep waiting for him to walk through that door and say 'Dougie, where are we eating lunch today?'"

"Mr. Hermann, I was hoping you could help me. I'm trying to find out exactly what happened on Sunday morning. I need to find out who tampered with the pie."

His brows were smooth and neat as if they'd been drawn onto his face. They perked up. "Isn't that Ranger Braddock's job? I was expecting him to drop by yesterday. Maybe I'll see him today. My wife said he came by the house on Sunday afternoon looking for me, but I was out of town."

I sat forward. "You were out of town on Sunday?"

"That's right. Someone in the city was selling a used grader for a good price, so I rushed down the mountain to buy it before someone else snatched it up." His smile bordered on amused. "That's why you're here, right? To hear my alibi and find out if I killed Emery?"

I shrugged. "Like I said—my bakery's reputation is in trouble."

"As a business owner, I empathize. We get the occasional disgruntled customer and then they slam us with bad reviews, and we have to work hard to regain everyone's trust."

"I spoke to Wendell Symfield." Full honesty seemed to be working with Mr. Hermann.

Another amused smile. "Yes, Wendell was an especially unhappy customer. He rented machinery that he had no clue how to operate. We've changed some of our policies now. Certain machines can only be rented to professionals and contractors. No more weekend, at-home DIY projects." His phone rang, and he pressed the intercom button. "What's up, Deke?"

"I got the bulldozer running again if Mike wants to use it later."

"Thanks, Deke, you're a genius." He took his finger off the button and rested back in his chair. "Look, I can see how important this is to you, so I don't mind giving you all the details of my morning. I left home at six. It took longer than usual to get to the city because I was dragging a twenty-foot trailer behind the truck. I got to the man's house at around nine and paid him for the grader. Then I left my trailer at his place while I did some errands and had lunch. I got back to his place around two, loaded the grader and then made the long, slow drive back up the hill to the excavation lot. I got back here around five in the evening. The grader is sitting in our B yard if you'd like to see it."

There was a small flaw in his purported alibi. "You were out running errands and having lunch? Didn't your wife call to let you know that Emery was dead?"

"You're good at this detective stuff. Yes, she left a message to call her, but she didn't want to leave the news in a voicemail or text, so I took my time calling her back. I finally did just as I was getting ready to drive back up the mountain. I can tell you I was in such a state of shock, I had to sit in the truck for a long time and process all of it. I guarantee you I was upset. At that time, it was assumed that he died of a heart attack. Emery had a bad heart and never took proper care of his health. I suppose that lessened the shock. But hearing that he'd been poisoned reignited all the disbelief."

"You are now the sole owner of the company," I noted.

His smooth brows did a dance. "You've been doing your homework, although I can't imagine how you would know that." Before I could answer, he snapped his fingers. "June, of course, she would know. I haven't had a chance to talk with her, but I plan to visit her later. And to counter your earlier accusation—"

This time my brows hopped up.

"Well, I suppose it wasn't an accusation. More like a point of interest, a detail that would give me clear motive. There will be some paperwork and other legalities to go through, but yes, I'll be the owner of the company. That had been Emery's idea. He had no family, and he was leaving June his property. His only stipulation was that his name remain on the company. Of course, I'm happy to keep it. Wouldn't be the same without his name on the sign. Now, if there's nothing else"—he waved his clean, manicured hand over the pile of folders on his desk—"I have a lot of work to do."

"Of course. Thank you for your time." I walked out of the hut. I glanced around the yard. I had no idea what a grader looked like, but his alibi sounded pretty solid. It seemed I'd hit another dead end.

thirty

...

I GOT BACK to the bakery, and business hadn't improved. "I suppose I can make a trip down to the soup kitchen when we close. They'll appreciate all these treats," Jack said.

"That's a great idea. We don't normally have anything left by the end of the day, but it looks as if we're going to have trays of goodies when we lock up. Why don't you take your lunch, Jack? I'm going to stay here and do some office work."

"I gather your visit to Gladstone's company didn't bear fruit." Jack took off his apron.

"Doug Hermann, who had great motive, also has a pretty solid alibi." I poured myself a cup of coffee to eat with one of my many leftover pastries.

"Pretty solid?" he asked.

"Well, he said he left town early to head down to the city. Someone was selling a grader at a good price, and he wanted to buy it before someone else did. It all sounded very plausible, and it meant he was nowhere near Ripple Creek the morning of the murder. Only, I suppose, there's always a chance that he made the whole story up. He's had time to come up with a good one. Dalton went to his house on Sunday afternoon, but Mrs. Gladstone told him Doug was out of town."

"She could have been in on the whole thing," Jack suggested.

"That's where my mind went, too. Mostly because it had nowhere else to go. I've talked to a few suspects, and no one is jumping out as the culprit."

"Well, if you want to start crossing people off, all you need to do to take Hermann off the list is look for an advertisement of a well-priced grader and see if it sold. Maybe you can even find out who bought it and when."

"Hmm, sort of a convoluted way to verify an alibi but I'll give it a try. In the meantime, have a good lunch. And try not to fret. I'll do all of that for the both of us."

Jack's deep, raspy chuckle followed him out the door.

I took my coffee and a sticky cherry Danish to the office and sat at the computer. There were several advertising sites to look at for construction equipment. After browsing a few dozen pages of everything from bulldozers to mini-tractors, I stumbled upon a grader, a massive yellow machine that looked as if it could flatten a mountain. The price had been "slashed for a quick sale," and there was nothing on the ad that indicated the machine had been sold. That didn't always mean much. I called the number.

"Joe's Landscaping, no job too big or too small. How can I help you?"

"Hello, I saw your advertisement for a grader online, and I was wondering if you still had it."

He laughed. "I could have sold that thing a dozen times already. I told my clerk to pull down the ad, but she must have

A Pie For A Pie

gotten busy. Someone came out Sunday morning to buy it. It's long gone. Sorry about that."

"No problem. You wouldn't by any chance know the name of the person who bought it? I'd like to see if he's interested in selling it."

"Gee, don't remember his name. He paid cash. He said he owned an excavation company. Sorry, I can't help you with that."

"No problem. Goodbye." I hung up and clicked out of the ad page. Doug Hermann's alibi had just gone from semi-solid to solid. The door to the bakery opened. It had been such a quiet day, I almost forgot to react. I got up and walked to the front.

I was hoping to find a group of locals with apologetic grins waiting to buy a dozen pastries. Instead, a young man I'd never seen before was glancing down at the clipboard in his hand. "Afternoon. Everything looks delicious."

"What can I get you?" I asked.

"Actually, I was hoping you could help me. I'm collecting signatures on this petition to recall councilwoman Ingrid Engalls. She is the only vote standing in the way of the new housing development off Lone Creek Highway."

I quickly deduced he was one of those people who got paid for each signature they collected. I'd heard about the proposed development. It had caused no small amount of debate in town, but I'd been so busy with the business, I hadn't had time to learn more about it. I certainly had no idea that Ingrid Engalls was in danger of being recalled. Nana was usually up on that kind of political gossip. I would have to ask her about it later.

I smiled politely. "I'm sorry. I need to learn more about it before I sign a petition."

He had a very white smile. "Are you sure you want to stand in the way of progress?" He glanced at his clipboard where he had a piece of paper with a script tucked under the clip. This young man couldn't have cared less about the reason for the petition. He was just looking for signatures. "The housing development will bring more people to the mountain, and that will be good for business." As he gave me his sales pitch, I wondered who was paying to get these signatures for the recall. I could only assume it was the real estate developer behind the new housing.

"Like I said, I won't sign until I know more about the issue. Are you sure I can't interest you in a brownie or cookie? We're having a two for the price of one sale." It was a sale I just started due to the abundance of leftovers on my shelves.

"Yeah, two for one? Then I'll take two brownies, please."

I saw the opportunity for important small talk as I packed his brownies. "Who is behind this recall?"

He looked surprised by the question and, also, entirely clueless. "Uh, I'm not sure. Maybe the businesses that are trying to build the development."

"I think you're probably right about that." I handed him the brownies and sent him and his clipboard on his way. My intuition told me I needed to dig deeper into the recall. Ingrid Engalls had never been on my suspect list. She had access to the pies, but she had no motive for killing Emery Gladstone. I certainly had no idea that her position on the council was in danger. I needed to know more, and my source was across the street in her giftshop. The day was slow enough that I didn't mind taping a sign to the door that said back in five minutes. I locked up and hurried across to Regina's shop. She was hanging Christmas ornaments on a wire.

"Scottie, I didn't expect to see you in here." She waved at the ornaments, shiny brown bears wearing holiday sweaters and holding tiny spruce trees. "What do you think? I saw them in the supplier's catalogue and just had to buy some."

"Very cute and mountainy. Regina, do you know anything about the town trying to recall Ingrid Engalls?"

Regina was always anxious to share gossip. Her eyes sparkled with enthusiasm. "I sure do. Ingrid has been the deciding vote on some hideous development a contractor is trying to build off Lone Creek Highway. It's one of those eyesore, cookie cutter communities where every house looks the same. Most of us are dead set against it, including Ingrid. She's been the holdout vote, so now people are trying to get her removed from the council."

"Do you know who's behind the recall?"

Regina hung the last bear and then pursed her lips in thought. "Gosh, I just assumed it was the developer. I'm sure he's got the backing of some of the building contractors in the area. It would have been a lucrative project for them."

I nodded. "It would indeed. Thanks. It seems I have some research to do."

Regina's posture perked up. "Oh? Are you trying to help Ingrid?" she asked.

"Uh, sure, I'm trying to get to the bottom of this recall. See you later." I headed back across the street and pulled my phone out as I reached the shop. Dalton's phone went to voicemail.

"Just wondering if you got the results on the turkey baster and little sidenote—did you know that there is an effort to remove Ingrid Engalls from the city council? It seems she's been the main obstacle on a big housing development off Lone Creek. I suppose you probably already know about it, but I only just learned about the recall. Let me know what you found out about the baster."

I hung up and sat down at the computer. I needed to find out more about Ingrid's political woes. Were they enough to push her to murder?

thirty-one
. . .

I TAPPED around on the keyboard for a few minutes. There was some contentious discussion about the proposed development on the Neighborhood News site. Some people hailed Ingrid as a hero, and others complained that she was standing in the way of progress. I wasn't entirely sure which side I fell on. Developments tended to be bad for the eco-systems and traffic on the roads. At the same time, like the signature collector noted, they were good for business. If I was even able to salvage my business from this disaster. The one thing I couldn't find in my research was the money source for the recall. The land was owned by Rathmore Land and Development. That was the only name I could find related to the project.

The phone rang. It was Dalton. "Hey, thought you'd want to know the turkey baster tested positive for alkaloids from the belladonna plant. No fingerprints. The bulb and plastic tube had been wiped clean. Good work."

"Thanks for keeping me posted."

"I'd heard about the effort to recall Ingrid. I don't know much about it. Not sure if there's a connection or not. I'll look into it."

"Thanks, and no hurry except my business is completely dead, and I've got dozens of baked goods *languishing* on the shelves."

"Sorry to hear that, Scottie." The last time we spoke, Dalton was running high on adrenaline after his breakup with Crystal. He was much more subdued today.

"Do I dare ask how everything is going with you?" I asked.

"Well, it's dead silence from the Miramont camp, which, frankly, has me pretty freaked out."

"Like the 'calm before the storm' scenario?'"

"Exactly."

"Maybe they've just accepted it and decided to move on."

Dalton sighed heavily into the phone. "Wouldn't that be nice? I'll talk to you later."

"Yep. Bye."

The front door opened. "It's just me," Jack called. He'd returned from lunch, and I realized the cherry Danish wasn't going to hold me over.

"I'm going to walk across to the market for a sandwich. All this investigating is making me hungry."

Jack looked up as he tied on his apron. "Find out anything significant?"

I thought about the morning. "Well, possibly. I discovered that there's an effort to recall Ingrid Engalls over her objection to a proposed housing development. Actually, I can't claim it as a discovery. A young man walked in with a petition to sign."

"Ms. Engalls?" he asked, surprised. "I hadn't even considered her a suspect. She had access to all the pies. But do you think the recall is related?"

I released a dejected harrumph. "I have no idea. This is one of those cases with so many threads, I don't know which one to pull first. I'll be able to think better on a cheese sandwich. I'll be back soon."

Jack looked as if he had something important to ask.

"What is it? Tell me you know something important about the case," I said.

He shook his head. "No, it's not that. I'm just wondering how many brownies and cupcakes to bake for tomorrow considering today's business."

My shoulders slumped. "I hadn't even thought of that. We can't keep baking things if no one is going to buy them." I winced thinking about it. "Should we make half?" Just asking the question formed a knot in my stomach.

"That's probably a safe bet."

It was hard not to feel entirely deflated as I walked out the door. I'd worked hard to build up the bakery, and all it took was one bad pie (which was good when it left the building) to wipe away the progress. I stepped into the market. Marge Bivens was at the counter talking animatedly about how she bakes her turkey. She pulled a bag of chestnuts and three russet potatoes out of her basket. The next item she pulled from the basket grabbed my attention like a firework display. It was a brand-new turkey baster.

I headed straight to the counter. "Hello, Roxi. Hello, Marge. I guess turkey is in the air. I see you're buying a new turkey baster."

Marge lifted it as if she'd forgotten she was holding one. "Oh, the baster, right. The bulb on my old one cracked, so I had to throw it away." Her explanation sounded reasonable.

"How are things? Are your chickens happy?" I asked.

"Yes, although, I'm sorry it had to come to this for my hens to be safe and happy. If Emery had just put up a higher fence—" she started and then waved her hand. "I don't want to rehash all that. Emery is gone, and his dog is going to a new home, and my hens are free to wander the yard. Of course, who knows what the next owners will be like. And that pesky realtor was back this morning."

"What realtor is that?" I asked.

"Oh, Joe Turtle or Tuttle or whatever his name is. He always has his face plastered everywhere. That's how I know it was him."

Roxi looked at me. "Guess June isn't wasting any time getting the place on the market."

"Does seem fast," I said. I walked to the sandwich refrigerator and pulled out a cheese and veggie on sourdough. Marge was on her way out as I reached the counter. Was the turkey baster just a coincidence? I was sure that Nana had been using the same baster for years. They were a kitchen tool you only took out occasionally for a turkey or a roast. But the bulbs were rubber, and rubber could get dry and crack.

"Roxi, did you know there was a petition going around to recall Ingrid Engalls from the council?"

"That kid cornered you, too? He had a nice little sales pitch to go with it. Far as I know that recall is never going to happen. Most locals are on Ingrid's side."

"You don't happen to know who's behind the recall efforts?"

"I heard it was the developer and some of the local contractors. I suppose that makes sense since they're the ones who would benefit from a big housing development. Has Dalton found out who poisoned Emery Gladstone?"

"Not yet."

Roxi counted back my change and peered up at me with a motherly look.

"So, you noticed that I had no customers this morning," I said.

"Looks a little quiet on your side of the street." She added a sympathetic grin to her motherly look. "I'm sure this will pass. There's no way this town is going to go *cold turkey* on Scottie's pastries. Everyone loves your treats and your breads."

"Thanks. I hope you're right." A truck motor rattled the front window. It was one of the Hermann and Gladstone trucks. It had a trailer behind it with a bulldozer loaded on the back. The driver walked into the market. It was Zach, the young worker who'd left a cold can of beer at the impromptu memorial for Emery.

"I hope you've still got some roast beef and cheese sandwiches back there, Roxi. I'm starved."

Roxi laughed airily, and it bordered on flirtatious. "There are probably a few left…just for you."

I turned back to Roxi with an arched brow. She blushed and waved off my look. I had to look past the cute and unusual reaction from my dear friend, Roxi. I needed information, and I was hoping Zach would have it.

He came up to the counter holding not two but three sandwiches. "I'll bet you were a hard teenager to keep fed," Roxi said with a giggle.

"Yes, I was. I could eat an entire pizza in one sitting." He smiled at me and reached for his wallet.

"You're Zach, right?" I asked. "I saw you leaving a memorial beer for Emery Gladstone at the park."

Zach had a thin layer of dirt covering his entire face, but it didn't detract from his looks. I could see why Roxi had a permanent blush as she rang him up.

"Zach, this might seem like an off-the-wall question, but do you happen to know whether or not the excavation company was going to be hired for the big housing development on Lone Creek?"

He handed Roxi his money and threw in a wink. "Yeah, we were slated to do all the excavation. It would have been a huge job, but I guess there's some kind of hold up with the city council. I don't know. I don't get too involved with that stuff. I just drive to where they tell me to go and collect my paycheck at the end of the week. Still, I think Mr. Gladstone was really upset that the whole thing had been delayed and possibly put on hold permanently."

"Interesting. Well, enjoy your sandwiches, and Roxi, I'll see you later." I walked out with my sandwich and a bit more information than when I walked in. The only problem now was tying any of that information to the killer.

thirty-two
. . .

JACK and I glumly mixed brownie batter and measured out starter for tomorrow morning's bread. My mind wasn't on the baking. It was on the investigation. I was breaking eggs into a container and managed to lose not one but two to the floor. After the second one, Jack chuckled.

"I can clean that up and finish these tasks. Why don't you take a break?"

I started taking off my apron. "I'm really in a fog today. So much has happened in the past few days that I can't keep a solid thought in my head."

"It always helps me to write down things when my thoughts are fuzzy," Jack suggested.

"You know what? You're right. I need to gather everything on paper." The front door opened. My mouth dropped. "Could it be a customer?"

"There's only one way to find out." Jack had his hands full with a mixing paddle and rubber scraper. He was looking for a place to set them down.

"Don't worry. I'll take care of it. I think I can pull myself from the muddle long enough to help a customer." I walked to the front and was surprised to find Thomas Anderson standing in the bakery. He was holding one of the canvas bags that Esme sold in her bookshop. It was loaded down with new books. "Thomas, how are you?"

His expression turned serious. "The question is—how are you? I was in the bookshop, and a few people were commenting that they were avoiding the bakery because of the pie incident. That doesn't seem fair. I thought I'd stop in and buy some treats for home."

"That's very kind of you, Thomas, and it's your lucky day because I'm selling everything at half price." I picked up a pink box and waited for him to make his selection. He dropped the handle of the bag over his arm.

"Looks like you've been buying some books," I said.

"Yep, I'm a big nature enthusiast. I've got dozens of books about flora and fauna. Always been a big hobby of mine. It's one of the reasons I moved up here. There's such an abundance of nature." He pulled one of the books out of the bag. It was a beautifully illustrated book about plants of the tropics. Just when I wasn't looking for it—I found another thread.

"That's a lovely book. I guess it tells you everything you need to know about each plant." Like how poisonous they are, I thought wryly. "You know, I recently met a man who has a gorgeous greenhouse."

Thomas smiled. "Hector Granger? He's a good friend. We exchange articles and talk every once in a while." He took a deep breath as he looked at the pastries. "I'll take a dozen pastries, mixed assortment, and a brownie for the road."

"You bet." It was nice of Thomas to buy so many treats. I was sure he didn't need that many. I packed the box and sent Thomas off with his baker's dozen and brownie for the road. It seemed innocent enough that he just happened to be a big flora and fauna enthusiast, but it also meant that he knew a lot about plants. He was also friends with Hector Granger, which meant he probably knew that Hector had belladonna growing in his greenhouse.

I returned to the kitchen. Jack was humming along to the radio as I waved and continued through to my office. I opened my notepad, picked up a pen and decided to start over with my earlier notes about Emery's murder. I had a list of names, starting with June Greene. She had a good motive. Emery refused to commit, and his death meant she inherited his valuable piece of property. She was at the park before the contest, and she bought flowers from Hector Granger. She seemed genuinely sad about Emery's death, but when we spoke, she acted as if selling the place was the last thing on her mind. But a realtor was already out looking at the property, so she must have been more anxious to sell it than she let on.

Thomas Anderson had motive, too, and I wasn't considering his desire to win the contest as part of that motive. His business took a huge hit when Emery's company decided to rent out big equipment. Of course, that happened two years earlier, so it seemed like a delayed reaction. On top of that, there were two partners in the company. Why only kill Emery? It certainly doesn't help Thomas recoup his losses. Thomas was at the park all morning, but he had an alibi for earlier in the morning when the pie was tampered with. He also knew a lot about native plants and was friends with Hector Granger.

Marge Bivens. I wrote the name and stared at it. I couldn't

believe I was having to include sweet Marge Bivens on the list. But Marge had motive. Emery had refused to keep his dog away from her hens, and from what Hannah said, it had been a constant source of stress and worry for Marge. She was buying a new turkey baster, claiming her old one broke. But was she really buying it to replace the one she hid in the park?

Doug Hermann had motive. He was now the sole owner of the excavation company. But he had a good alibi that I'd confirmed with my call about the grader. I decided to cross him off the list before I got overwhelmed with suspects.

Wendell Symfield had motive, too. His house had been badly damaged by the machine he'd rented from Emery's company, but when I spoke to him, he seemed to have accepted the judge's decision that the company owed him nothing. However, belladonna was growing in his neighbor's greenhouse, so it would have been easy for him to take a few cuttings of the poisonous plant. But again, why only Emery? Two men owned the excavation company. I'd never gotten around to whether or not Wendell was at the park on Sunday morning. I certainly didn't remember seeing him.

That left Ingrid Engalls. She was a surprise addition to the list. Of course, she had access to the pies, and she was alone with those same pies for a portion of the morning. She saw to that because she told Diedre, her assistant, that she didn't need to get to the park until an hour before the contest. Was Ingrid making sure she had time to tamper with the pies? As far as motive went, it was somewhat convoluted. She'd obviously been having some problems on the council and had angered a number of people who'd been counting on the housing development that she'd opposed. And there was one small detail that came to me as I was writing the list. Ingrid's kitchen was filled with fresh herbs, and her assistant, Diedre, mentioned that Ingrid was sipping her herbal tonic because she was very stressed about the contest. Or was she stressed because she already knew the shocking ending? If Ingrid was into herbal tonics, then there was a good chance she knew Hector Granger and his greenhouse of leafy wonders.

I put down the pen and shook out my hand. "Wow, what a list."

"What's that?" Jack called from the kitchen.

I got up from the desk and joined him at the work counter. He was busy weighing out flour for the bread. "I've got a long list of suspects, and I've really only crossed one off the list—Emery's partner, Doug Hermann. I took your advice and called about the grader. The seller said a man who owned an excavation company bought it Sunday morning. His clerk hadn't taken the ad down yet."

"Sounds like you can cross him off." Jack pushed the scale aside and closed up the flour bin. "Are you leaning toward any of the people on the list?"

"I thought I was, several times. Then another detail would pop up, and I'd find myself back at the beginning. Usually, I'm on to something by now. I don't have time to keep running circles around the list, and the bakery certainly can't have more days like this."

"What about Ranger Braddock? Maybe he's having better luck."

"Let's hope so." I picked up some of the mixing bowls and carried them to the sink. Something told me Dalton wasn't putting a hundred percent into this investigation. He had too many other things on his mind. After I cleaned up, I planned to go through everything on the list one more time, then I'd call

Dalton to see if he was any closer. With any luck, he'd call me in the meantime to let me know he'd made an arrest.

"I'm finished measuring out bread ingredients." Jack carried the flour sack to the back and returned. "I guess I'll start boxing up the leftovers to take to the soup kitchen."

"That's a good idea." I placed the mixing bowl in the soapy water. "Let's hope our fortunes change tomorrow."

thirty-three
. . .

AFTER READING and rereading my notes, I decided to visit Ingrid Engalls. The first few times I'd spoken to her, I hadn't even considered her a suspect. I just wanted details of that morning, and she was happy to provide them. There was nothing about her expression when I spoke to her that made me think she was guilty, but that didn't mean much. Even though Ingrid had the easiest opportunity to poison Emery's pie, it never occurred to me that she was the killer. She had no motive, and the whole, tragic event was a disaster for the town and city council. It seemed unthinkable that she would sabotage an event that she had planned, but the recall effort meant Ingrid had motive. Zach said Emery's company was in line for the excavation contract, a huge job for Gladstone and Hermann Excavation. I was sure they were contributing money to the recall effort. What didn't make sense was—why only go after Emery? Why not Doug Hermann? Why not the actual developer?

The late afternoon sky was gray with a set of clouds that had floated in and anchored themselves on the surrounding peaks. The chill in the air had hints of snow. I drove to Ingrid's house. Her car was in the driveway. I wasn't entirely sure how to go about questioning her. She was certainly not expecting me, and I wasn't sure how she'd react to my visit. I'd brought along a few pastries hoping to sweet treat my way inside.

I rang the doorbell, and she came to the door in her apron. The smell of onions and garlic wafted past her to the front stoop. "Hmm, something smells delicious," I said.

That made her smile. "It's my beef stew. I always make it when the weather turns cold."

"Sounds like the perfect meal for a chilly autumn night." I glanced back toward the gray sky. "Looks like we might get a sprinkling of snow."

"Then the stew will taste even better." Pleasantries over with, Ingrid tilted her head in question. "Why are you here?"

I held out the box of pastries. "I was hoping to ask you a few questions. You see, my bakery is in trouble now because of the contest, and I'm trying to get to the bottom of it before my business goes belly-up."

Ingrid was wearing a fluffy white turtleneck, and a few of the fluffy hairs tickled her neck. She swiped at them quickly. "I'm not sure how I can help, Scottie. I'm very sorry about your bakery business, but we need to wait for Ranger Braddock to make an arrest. Then all of this will work itself out. Thank you for the pastries." She moved to close the door.

"Is it true there's a petition to have you recalled from the city council?" She was about to shut the door on me, but I lobbed that little grenade first and it worked.

Her mouth dropped into a frown. Another piece of her fluffy sweater broke free and temporarily tickled her nose. She wiggled it back and forth and then returned to her frown. "It's a pathetic attempt to intimidate me into voting yes, but it's not going to work." She stood up straighter and launched into a well-practiced political speech. "I work hard for this community. The new development will damage important ecosystems and clog our streets with traffic."

I held up a hand. "It's all right, Ingrid. I'm on your side, and it takes courage for you to remain steadfast even when being faced with a recall."

She relaxed some and pushed the turtleneck down lower on her neck. "Thank you. I think most of the locals feel the same." She squinted at me for a second. "Is that why you're here? You heard that Gladstone and Hermann Excavation were part of the recall effort, so you thought I killed Emery?"

I hadn't expected such a direct question. "No, well, I mean, well—look, I don't think you killed Emery. I'm just trying to gather some facts." She hadn't invited me in, so it seemed I was going to have to toss out the next question from the front stoop. "Do you buy your herbs from Hector Granger?"

She looked baffled and rightfully so. "Who? Hector Granger? Wait, I know that name. He had to get permission from the council to build a very large greenhouse on his small property. What about him? And, to answer your question, no, I buy my herbs from the farmer's market near the resort. There's a couple there who grow marvelous herbs and sell bundles at good prices. How does this connect to Emery's death?" It was a reasonable question, and since my intuition was telling me the woman across the threshold was not a killer, I decided to fill her in.

"Emery's pie was laced with poison from the Atropa belladonna plant. It's a plant that thrives in warm humidity, and

Hector grows it in his greenhouse. He also had someone break into the greenhouse on Saturday night."

Ingrid's eyes grew wide with comprehension. "So, the killer stole some of his plant. Then they would've had to know that Hector grew the poisonous plant. How did you know about it?" she asked with a quick turn of the tables. She was good. It was easy to see why people always voted her onto the council.

"I was talking to Wendell Symfield about his lawsuit against the excavation company, and Hector walked over to tell Wendell about the break-in."

Ingrid nodded approvingly. "You've really been deep into this. I know about Wendell's lawsuit. I believe it was dismissed."

"It was, and he seemed disappointed but accepting of that outcome. And as for being deep in this—I'm trying to save my bakery."

"Of course, and I hope this all gets cleared up soon."

"Well, I'll let you go. Enjoy the pastries." I turned to walk away.

"You know—"

I turned back.

"It seems to me that whoever did this—they had a bone to pick with Emery. Not with the company. Otherwise, why only kill Emery? Doug Hermann is co-owner of the excavation company."

"Actually, he's sole owner now. He inherits Emery's share of the company."

Ingrid looked stunned. "My goodness, that's quite a windfall. Have you spoken to—"

I nodded. "Yes, Doug had motive. He also has an alibi. He was in the city on Sunday morning."

"I see. Well, again, I'm sure Ranger Braddock will make an

arrest soon and then everyone will be anxious to buy your baked goods again."

"I sure hope so. Thanks for talking to me." I walked to the car and was happy to get out of the cold. A few tiny flakes fell from the gray sky, but not enough to coat anything. I tapped my steering wheel as I thought about what Ingrid said. It was the same question I'd been asking myself all along. If someone was angry at the company, then why would they just go after Emery? And if it wasn't Doug Hermann, then the killer had to be someone who was upset with Emery and only Emery. That left two people—Marge Bivens and June Greene.

thirty-four
· · ·

THE SNOWFLAKES GOT HEAVIER, and the sky grew darker, but I had things to do. Nana would be worried, so I called her first. "Button, is that you?" Even though my name was on the screen, she always asked that when she answered the phone, and I found it adorable. She told me it came from growing up with telephones that rang, and you had no idea who would be on the other end until you answered it.

"Yes, Nana, I wanted to let you know I'd be a little late. I've already locked up the bakery for the day."

"I've made some lentil soup for dinner, so don't be too long."

"Hmm, that sounds good. It's been a long day, and the snow is falling, so hot soup will be perfect. I'll see you soon."

Before I could hang up, she asked another question. "Should we invite Dalton? Regina called me earlier, and she said Dalton and Crystal had broken up. I figured he could use some friendly faces and hot soup."

I huffed. I had no idea how I was going to break Nana's habit of constantly inviting Dalton to meals. "Nana, he's fine. He broke it off. Not her. I think it would be easier for me if we didn't have him over to the house so often." There was silence on her end. "Nana? Don't be angry."

"No, I'm not, Button. And you're right. You're starting a relationship with Cade, and if having Dalton over makes that harder, then I won't invite him as much. It's only that I feel bad for him."

"I know and I'm not saying you have to stop inviting him. Just less often. By the way, he considers you his best friend. Just like I consider you my best friend."

"That's sweet, Button. I'll see you soon. Don't be too late."

"I won't." My phone rang just as I hung up. It was Dalton.

"Hey, any news?" I asked, hopefully.

"No, because I got called up to the resort. Several cars were broken into, and I didn't dare ignore the request. I need Miramont to see that he needs me up here and that I do a good job."

I giggled. I was tired and that sometimes made me get ornery. "Are you sure Crystal didn't break into those cars herself?" I gasped. "Sorry, that was uncalled for."

"Actually, that very notion crossed my mind more than once. But supposedly Crystal was shopping in the city with her mom. I'm sure she bought up half the stores. She shops whenever she's unhappy."

"Wow, I'll bet the boutique owners in the city had a bountiful day. Unlike a certain baker. Jack took almost our entire inventory down to the soup kitchen."

"At least there'll be some very happy people at the soup kitchen."

"That's true, and it makes the whole failed day a little easier to swallow."

Soft, white flakes were starting to collect on my windshield. I needed to get moving. I planned to visit Marge Bivens first.

"What about you? Did you find anything else about Emery's death? By the way, there is little chance of that recall effort taking hold, so I don't think we need to worry about Ingrid," Dalton said.

"I agree. I've got a whole chart with suspects and motives and proximity to both the poisonous plant and the pie contest, but Ingrid said something to me after I spoke to her. She said it seemed if someone had a beef with the excavation company, then there were two owners. Why kill Emery if Doug was just going to move on with the business?"

"That's true. So, you're thinking—"

I hated to admit but I loved it when he asked my advice on a case. How could I ever push Dalton a hundred percent from my life when I spent so much time on these cases? "I'm thinking the killer had one pure goal in mind—kill Emery Gladstone. This has nothing to do with the company."

"Sounds like we can get this narrowed down then," he said.

"We? I like that. And with you stuck at the resort, I'm going to head over to Marge Bivens' house. It's impossible to think she could have done something so heinous, but she had motive, and she freely admits her life is better now that Emery is gone. And, get this—she was buying a new turkey baster at the market this afternoon."

"Hmm, never arrested someone for buying a turkey baster, but you might be on to something. Just be careful. Remember, I'm the official who gets to charge and arrest the suspect."

"I see. So, I do the work, and you get to have all the fun and glory."

He chuckled. It was always a good sound coming through

the phone. It seemed he was feeling better after his breakup. "Trust me, there's nothing glorious or fun about investigating a car break-in. I'm almost done here, and it looks like we're getting snow, so don't stay out long."

"It's just a few flakes. I'll keep you posted. Bye." I started the car and drove to Marge's house. A light glowed in her front window, and her roof was powdered with snow.

The yard was empty. I assumed her beloved hens were tucked in for the night. I knocked on the front door. Marge lifted the curtains on her door and peered out. She looked somewhat frightened about the prospect of someone knocking on her door. It was getting dark out, so I couldn't blame her. I lowered my face and waved. It took her a second to recognize me. She smiled and opened the door.

"Scottie, I certainly wasn't expecting to find you standing at my front door. Come in, quick. It's very cold outside."

I stomped my shoes to shake free the flakes and brushed off my coat before entering. There was a bouquet of flowers sitting on an antique walnut table in the entryway. Before I could ask where she bought her flowers, I got a closer look and realized they were fake.

"Will you have a cup of hot tea? I just put the kettle on. I find it helps take the chill off." She adjusted her knit shawl around her shoulders. "I hadn't expected snow or a visitor. Otherwise, I would have started a fire."

"A cup of tea would be nice." I followed her into her kitchen. The backsplash was covered in cheery red and white tile, and there were matching red and white canisters lining the counter.

Marge walked to the canisters. "I've got some new peppermint tea. Or maybe some apple cinnamon?"

"Whatever you're having," I said as I sat at the table.

"I like peppermint at this time of day." Peppermint filled the air as she pulled two tea bags out of one of the canisters.

Marge sat down across from me as we waited for the kettle. Her cheeks rounded like pink apples. "I'm so pleased you're here. I don't get many visitors."

I felt like a heel. How could I possibly consider this sweet woman was involved in Emery's murder?

"I wanted to ask you a few questions about your neighbor, Emery."

"What about poor Emery? I mean I had such a time with that man, and now I feel bad that we weren't nicer to each other." The kettle whistled, and Marge hopped up to pour the water. She set the tea in front of me and sat with her own cup. "What do you want to know about him?"

Suddenly, it wasn't Emery I was interested in. It was June. "How often did you meet or talk to June Greene?"

Her brows were flecked with gray. "Gosh, not that often. Since Emery and I weren't on speaking terms, I didn't get a chance to talk to June much. She seemed nice enough, and I did hear her one day telling Emery he should raise the fence. Why do you ask?"

"I was hoping to hear a little more about her relationship with Emery. Did you hear them arguing much?"

Marge thought about it as she blew on her tea. "There's quite a bit of distance between our houses, but I did see her leave his place on Saturday afternoon in a huff. She marched out to her car. He called her name, but she ignored him and drove off."

I wondered if that was the ultimatum conversation. Emery had brushed off the whole threat. It almost sounded as if he'd found it too meaningless to consider.

"You mentioned that a realtor, Mr. Tuttle, was snooping

around the property today."

"That's right. I guess he can't wait to get his 'For Sale' sign out front. It wasn't the first time he's driven past."

I took a sip of tea, and my face popped up. "What do you mean?"

"He drove by last week, Monday, I think it was. He was sitting out front looking at his phone, so I walked right out and asked him what he was doing," Marge said with a chin lift.

"What did he say?" I asked.

"Just that he was looking at the property next door and that he'd be leaving soon. He took off after that."

"Was Emery looking to sell his house?" I asked.

"Not that I know of, but then, he wouldn't have told me if he was."

We both sipped our tea. I was trying to be polite and enjoy the tea, but I badly wanted to move ahead with my investigation. I needed to see June Greene. Why was a realtor checking out a property when it wasn't on the market? Was June trying to get a value for a house she'd inherit if Emery died?

"Just out of curiosity, Marge," I asked. "What do you think Emery's property is worth?"

Marge's cheeks rounded again. "These properties have become extremely valuable in the past few years. I'm not sure why, but I had a realtor call to let me know he could sell this place for a million dollars. Isn't that ridiculous?" She glanced around at her tiny kitchen. "Can you imagine that?"

"It's a beautiful location, and the flat acreage is hard to find in the mountains, so I can see it, yes." I finished my tea. "Thank you so much. It was just what I needed."

Marge walked me to the door. "Please, stop by any time."

I felt bad rushing off, but I was hot on the trail of a killer.

thirty-five
. . .

I SAT in the car and weighed my options. I couldn't go straight to June's house and accuse her of murder without more evidence. As Marge had mentioned, Joe Tuttle, the realtor, had his face plastered all over the place. It was easy to find his contact number. I dialed it, and he answered enthusiastically on one ring. "Joe Tuttle here, to take care of all your house buying needs. With whom do I have the pleasure of speaking today?"

"Hello, my name is Scottie, and I'm interested in a property on Meadowlark Lane. A friend told me it would be going on the market soon."

"Oh, yes, June Greene's property." He was already referring to her as the owner. "There will be a slight delay on selling that property. It's an inheritance, you see, and there are still some legalities to smooth out before we can list it. It's a prime property though, and you're smart to get your name in early. I expect it to go quickly."

"Oh really. That's interesting. A friend of mine lives on the street, and she said you were already out there last week looking at the property."

He cleared his throat. "Well, it's not official yet, but yes, it's true, Ms. Greene, asked me to look at the property last week to get an idea of the value. I must tell you it'll be priced at a million dollars. I'm not sure if you're looking for that price point. If not, I have other properties to look at."

"I'm mostly interested in that specific property. Thanks for your time."

"Wait, I can contact you as soon as it's on the market," he said anxiously, worried he'd lose a potential client.

"You're right. The price is a little out of my range. I'll think about looking elsewhere. Thanks. Goodbye." I hung up quickly. The snowflakes had grown in size and volume, but since it was the first snow of the season, the flakes weren't sticking to the road. It was dark now, but I had one more important stop. First, I had a phone call to make and a little bragging was in order.

It went to Dalton's voicemail. "Hello, it's your brilliant, sidekick partner. That's what I'm calling myself now. Of course, I'll need a confession to make a hundred percent sure, but my money is now on June Greene as the killer. I'll tell you how I know that when I see you. I'm heading to her house now."

June had a small house just a mile from Emery's property. Although it wasn't Emery's property anymore. It belonged to June, and she was pricing the place at least a week before she inherited it. Maybe she was making sure it was valuable enough to be worth her time and effort to plot and carry out a murder.

Smoke curled up from June's chimney as I walked up the brick path to her front door. A big wreath with silk leaves and a red bow hung on the front door. She'd already brought out her holiday decorations, and a light-up snowman smiled up at me around his black pipe as I reached the porch.

It seemed everyone had gotten the urge to cook tonight. First snows did that to people. Something smelled quite tasty as she opened the door. She was usually dressed in tight jeans and sweaters, but tonight she was wearing sweatpants and her hair was in a ponytail.

"Scottie," she said it with a sort of pained look on her face. Then she forced a smile. "Hello." She glanced past me to the street where I'd parked my car. "Are you lost?"

"Nope, I'm pretty sure I'm at the right house."

She stared at me for a second. Her bottom lip started to quiver, so she took a deep breath to collect herself. "You'll have to excuse me. I'm just about to sit down to dinner."

"You almost got away with it, but greed got in your way," I said. I was tired and hungry and not in the mood to dance around waiting for a confession.

Her lip quivered again, and she blinked away some tears. "I don't know what you're talking about. It's late. Don't you have some cupcakes to frost?" she said curtly.

"No, because you've ruined the reputation of my bakery with your murder stunt."

Some of the color drained from her face. "I don't know what you're talking about."

"I'm talking about your murder of Emery Gladstone. You should have at least waited until Emery was dead before you had a realtor out to give the property a look."

Her mouth hung open and more color drained from her face.

"You should probably sit down," I said and took her arm. I stepped inside and led her to the couch.

She sat with a plunk and immediately covered her face and sobbed. It all seemed a touch dramatic for a woman who'd plotted a cold-blooded murder of her boyfriend. I was expecting a full confession, but I didn't get it.

She dropped her hands, and now her face was red with rage. The tears had miraculously dried up. "How dare you come into my house and accuse me of something so horrible? I loved Emery, and he loved me. We were going to make a beautiful life together."

"Only you gave Emery an ultimatum, and he wasn't interested in getting married. I heard you complaining about it in the market."

"You're just mad because your pie killed my poor Emery, and you don't want to take the blame for it. Obviously, your pie was bad."

I was really disappointed that she wasn't spilling out a confession. It was getting late, and I was dying for a bowl of Nana's lentil soup. "You shop at Hector Granger's greenhouse for flowers. You told me so yourself."

"A lot of people buy flowers from Hector. It means nothing." She wriggled on the seat cushion and pushed her posture straighter, apparently thinking that made her look more innocent.

"Face it—you have no evidence to accuse me. I made sure—" She paused and looked as if she'd just swallowed her own tongue.

I smiled. "You made sure not to leave prints or evidence. However, I did find your turkey baster."

"You can't prove it was mine."

"Right. And you know that because you took time to wipe it free of prints before stashing it under the rock."

There was a knock at the door. She looked startled by it, but then lifted her chin confidently. "I have a guest, so now it's time for you to leave and take your slanderous accusations elsewhere." She got up and waved me vigorously toward the door. She smoothed her hair and her sweater. It seemed she did have a guest. Was she already dating someone new?

"You need to go now," she said through gritted teeth. She pulled open the door and took a few stumbling steps back when she saw Ranger Braddock, hat, uniform and all, standing on her doorstep.

Dalton snuck me a lopsided smile and turned back to June with a serious brow. "June Greene, I'm going to need you to come to the station for questioning about the death of Emery Gladstone."

This time, June put on her best incredulous chin-drop. "Ranger Braddock, not you, too. Scottie has been running circles around herself trying to make me take responsibility for Emery's death. But there's no evidence."

Dalton stepped inside off the snowy porch. "Your fingerprints were found on a pair of garden shears in Hector Granger's greenhouse. He said someone broke into his greenhouse on Saturday night and took branches off an Atropa belladonna plant. The plant you used to poison Emery Gladstone."

June stumbled back with a look of disbelief. "Fingerprints? That's impossible. I wore gl—" She stumbled back farther but was stopped short by her couch.

"You wore gloves?" Dalton asked. "That's why we didn't find any prints. But we'll go down to the station now, so you can give me a full confession."

"No, I mean, that's not what I was going to say." This time her tears were real. "He strung me along for years telling me we were going to be married. I wasted so much time with him. I deserved to have that property."

Dalton calmly started reading her rights. I headed outside to wait for him to finish. Minutes later, June was dressed in her winter coat, and her face was as white as the snow in the garden. Dalton nodded to me. I got in the car. My work was done here, and lentil soup was waiting.

thirty-six
. . .

THE LAST PERSON I EXPECTED, but definitely the person I wanted to see, was sitting at Nana's table behind a steaming bowl of soup when I walked inside. My grandmother looked starry-eyed as Cade told her about his time in Rome. (I was sure the stars in her eyes had more to do with the way he looked in his black sweater than his description of the Colosseum.) Nana could barely pull her gaze from him when I stepped into the kitchen.

"Button, there you are. I hope you don't mind. I invited Cade for dinner. I made way too much soup for just the two of us."

Cade's smile was mild, and it made my knees jelly. "Evie is an incredible cook," he said.

Nana released a girly giggle; one I'd never heard before. "Are you ready for seconds?"

She reached for his bowl, but I put a hand on her shoulder. "I'll get it and serve one for myself."

Nana was fine with that. "So which European city did you

like the best?" she asked Cade. "I've heard Vienna is wonderful."

"Vienna is fantastic. Like something out of a painting," Cade said. I placed the soup in front of him. He winked at me, and my knees went weak again.

I sat down with my soup. It certainly felt different having Cade in our tiny kitchen, but something also felt right about it. He was a successful author, a man of the world and more sophisticated than anyone I'd ever met, but he looked exactly right sitting behind the bowl of soup.

"Button, did you find out who killed Emery Gladstone?" Nana asked.

I spotted a tiny bit of tension in Cade's jaw at the question. He knew that if I was out investigating, it meant I'd been interacting with Dalton. He wore a wry grin. "Yes, *Button*, do tell."

"First of all, there is only one person on this earth who is allowed to call me Button." I patted Nana's hand.

"I don't mind," Nana said.

"I do. And yes, I did catch the killer." I dipped my spoon into the soup, blew on it and took a bite. They were both watching me with interest.

I looked at each of them. "Oh, I guess you want to know who did it. June Greene, Emery's girlfriend," I said casually, as if the whole case already bored me. "It was a mix of spurned lover and greed. She was ready to sell his property before he was even cold in the grave. In fact, long before that. That's what gave her away." I picked up the salt shaker and tossed some into the soup.

"Well, aren't you clever," Nana said.

"Oh, it was nothing. All in a day's work of a bakery owner."

about the author

London Lovett is the author of the Port Danby, Starfire, Firefly Junction, Scottie Ramone and Frostfall Island Cozy Mystery series. She loves getting caught up in a good mystery and baking delicious, new treats!

Learn more at:
www.londonlovett.com

Printed in Great Britain
by Amazon